CONSPIRACY IN CRIME

elise sax

Copyright © 2020 by Elise Sax
All rights reserved.
ISBN: 979-8646983375
Published in the United States by 13 Lakes Publishing

Cover design: Elizabeth Mackey
Edited by: Novel Needs
Formatted by: Jesse Kimmel-Freeman

elisesax.com
elisesax@gmail.com
http://elisesax.com/mailing-list.php
https://www.facebook.com/ei.sax.9

ALSO BY ELISE SAX

Matchmaker Mysteries Series

*Matchmaking Advice
from Your Grandma
Zelda
Road to Matchmaker
An Affair to
Dismember
Citizen Pain
The Wizards of Saws
Field of Screams*

*From Fear to Eternity
West Side Gory
Scareplane
It Happened One
Fright
The Big Kill
It's a Wonderful
Knife
Ship of Ghouls*

Goodnight Mysteries Series

*Die Noon
A Doom with a View
Jurassic Dark
Coal Miner's
Slaughter
Wuthering Frights*

Agatha Bright Mysteries Series

*The Fear Hunter
Some Like It Shot
Fright Club*

Matchmaker Marriage Mysteries

Gored of the Rings

Partners in Crime Thrillers

*Partners in Crime
Conspiracy in Crime
Divided in Crime*

Operation Billionaire Trilogy
How to Marry a Billionaire
How to Marry Another Billionaire
How to Marry the Last Billionaire on Earth

Five Wishes Series
Going Down
Man Candy
Hot Wired
Just Sacked
Wicked Ride
Five Wishes Series

Three More Wishes Series
Blown Away
Inn & Out
Quick Bang
Three More Wishes Series

Standalone Books
Forever Now
Bounty
Switched

For Dolly, who keeps me company while I write.

CHAPTER 1

"Have you noticed that nobody's trying to kill us?"

No. Peter Bolton hadn't noticed anything except for Piper's long red hair that kissed her shoulders in thick waves, and her long eyelashes, which moved over her green, twinkling eyes.

That was a lie. He noticed other things, too.

Like her breasts. He noticed them. They were firm and high in her blue blouse, and he knew from personal experience that they fit perfectly into his large hands. And then there was all the rest about her, which he knew from personal experience, too. The way they fit together, for example. That was a good one. The way she looked at him when she was aroused.

Uh-oh. Speaking of aroused, he'd better think of

something else or he was going to make a scene in the tattoo removal clinic. They had come to remove the tattoo on the back of Piper's neck, a remnant of her abduction, which had left her an amnesiac.

"Clogged drains and Brussel sprouts," Peter replied.

Piper whipped her head around and studied his face. Her mouth scrunched up in the way she had when she was trying to figure something out. "Huh?"

"Clogged drains and Brussel sprouts don't arouse me," Peter said and smirked.

"Don't get me wrong," she continued as if Peter hadn't said anything. "It's fabulous that nobody's trying to kill us, but it's also a little sad. And boring."

"I like boring. I'm retired," Peter reminded her. He had been an international superspy, but he had given that up to fall in love with a beautiful and filthy rich woman. He had never been happier, even though they had almost been killed at least a dozen times since he had discovered her naked in the redwood forest a few weeks ago.

The technician entered the sterile room and instructed Piper to sit in a chair with her head forward. "Around forty-five million people in the United States have at least one tattoo," Piper informed the technician. It was her shtick to know trivia. She seemed to have an unlimited knowledge of little-known facts. The only thing she didn't know was who she was and where she was from.

Peter opened the passenger door of their Porsche Cayenne, and Piper climbed in. She watched him jog around the car and get into the driver's seat. "Does it hurt a lot?" he asked her, throwing a look to her neck.

"No, I'm happy that it's gone," she said honestly. If she couldn't remember the time during her abduction, it was fair that she didn't have to be reminded of it with an unwelcome tattoo.

Peter started the car, but she put her hand on his, urging him to turn off the motor.

"Are you all right?" he asked, concerned. "Are you getting a flashback of the abduction?"

Piper shook her head and trailed her fingers up his arm. "No, I was thinking of something far more serious."

"Murder? Mayhem? The end of the world?"

She unbuckled her seatbelt and climbed over his seat, where she straddled his lap. "No. I was wondering what it was like to have sex in a Porsche."

Peter's pupils dilated, and he arched an eyebrow.

"That's funny. I've often wondered the exact same thing."

Piper lifted his shirt and felt his hard abs. "In French, a six-pack is called a tablette de chocolat. A chocolate bar," she said, while she unbuttoned his pants, freeing his erection. She wrapped her hand around it, making Peter groan.

"Maybe we should give it a try," he croaked, barely able to get the words out. "Purely for scientific reasons."

"I do like to have a steady stream of data on hand," she said and brought her lips down hard on his.

Her body heated up to dangerous levels from the kiss, and she wondered vaguely if she could die like this, like a dog left in a car in a parking lot in Arizona. But it was only the end of June, and it was San Francisco, which hadn't gotten hot since they moved there a week before.

Sex was good with Peter. Not good… Great. Not great…perfect. At least, she thought it was perfect. She had amnesia, so he was the only sexual partner she remembered. But it was hard to contemplate sex being better than this.

It was the kind written in romance novels. He was always hard. She was always wet. They had done every position known, but they were more than happy with the missionary position.

Just like a romance novel.

They couldn't keep their hands off of each other, since they had finally come together in Bora Bora. It had already made for a few embarrassing moments, but Piper didn't care. She couldn't get enough of Peter.

And she was in love with him. Gaga, over the moon, unbridled in love with him.

Peter lifted Piper's skirt and guided her over him.

"Oh," she moaned. Her hips began to move over him.

Peter cupped her face with his hands. "Open your eyes, Piper. Look at me," he urged in an emotional whisper.

She opened her eyes and was greeted by the love in his. It was always like this between them. Connection. Unspoken communication.

Peter drove his body into hers, and her core yielded for him. She was short of breath, as her passion rose. She could feel Peter reaching toward his climax, too, and she kissed him again to hasten it.

Her skin sprouted goosebumps over every square inch, and her senses came alive. She was like a superhero or a magical being. She could see, smell, hear, taste, and touch like a superhuman. And it was all because Peter brought it out of her. His touch brought her to heights she hadn't thought possible. And his touch was everywhere. On her breasts, her lips, her ass. Inside her.

They moved together as if they were one with a singular goal between them, as if one was only a continuation of the other. Her core began to tighten, and the muscles rolled in a sweet physical response that began to take her away.

Ecstasy, she thought. Superhuman powers through ecstasy.

Piper's ecstasy was approaching fast. Her head dropped back, as she allowed her body to take over. Just like a self-driving car, she thought humorously. Her body didn't let her down. Led by a potent mix of pleasure and desire, it crossed a bridge of intense bow-chicka-wow-wow into a seizure-inducing happy ending.

"You drive me crazy," he moaned, as they climaxed together.

"You drive me crazy, too," she said. But he didn't drive her crazy. He grounded her, provided her with a foundation of love and security that she had become instantly addicted to and would defend to the death.

"So crazy." Peter breathed heavily into her ear. "I'm hearing bells."

Piper sat up straight and listened. "I'm hearing bells, too. It's your phone."

Piper climbed off of Peter and returned to the passenger seat. Peter dug his phone out of his pocket and looked at the screen. "Adesh," he said.

"Answer it."

"But I'm naked. I don't want to talk to Adesh while I'm naked."

"He won't know you're naked on the phone," Piper said, smoothing her hair, which had gone wild during their lovemaking.

Peter shuddered. "I'll know I'm naked, and I can't do that. Not with Adesh."

"You could always get dressed," she said, pointing at Peter's crotch.

"Oh," he said, sounding disappointed. "So, we're not going to go for another round?"

"No more car sex today. I don't want to get arrested."

Peter sighed and zipped his pants up. Once he was fully clothed, he answered the phone. "Yes, we're going to pick up Pop-Tarts on the way home," he said into the phone on speaker.

"Don't stop for anything. Come home immediately. There's an emergency!" Adesh yelled.

Peter got home in seven minutes. It wasn't a record for him, but it was pretty damned close. He and

Piper had bought a stately mansion, high atop San Francisco, and were still in the midst of moving in. They had bought the place with all of the staging furniture included, but they had been busy putting their own touches to it, including a weapons room, a panic suite, and enough information hardware for Adesh to start World War Three or take over Disney, if he so desired.

Adesh Sharma had done some freelance hacking work for Peter when he had been a spy, and since then, Peter and Piper had sort of adopted the four-hundred-pound computer science genius.

"Stay here," Peter ordered Piper when they parked in the driveway.

She laughed. "Ha! Funny one."

"Fine. C'mon, but stay behind me."

Peter pulled a pistol out of his ankle holster and got out of the car. He approached the house with caution, waiting for any sign of trouble. But there wasn't one. No obvious intrusion and no trespassers. Just Adesh's Bee Gees music blaring from the back of the house where his office was located.

Stayin' alive! Stayin' alive!

Peter paused at the front door and turned toward Piper. "I used to be a very impressive spy."

"You're still impressive."

"I'm expecting John Travolta to hop out in his

white suit. This is a step down from breaking into North Korea."

Piper patted his back. "I know. If you want, you can shoot the refrigerator later."

"Thanks, but I don't want to damage the cold cuts. I'm planning on making a sub sandwich later to eat with the game."

"You can't do that. We're going out tonight," Piper reminded him.

"Damn it. That's right."

He carefully opened the door and followed the music to Adesh, all the while watching for intruders. But everything looked exactly the way they left it. They found Adesh safe and sound in his office.

He was standing amidst the monitors and cords that he hadn't yet set up, and he was wearing only boxer shorts. When Peter and Piper entered, Adesh held up a suit jacket.

"Help," he pleaded. "The suit doesn't fit. Those bastard tailors don't know how to measure."

Peter ran his hand over his face in frustration. "Is that what this is about? A suit? I almost shot you."

Adesh threw the suit jacket on the floor and stomped his foot. "Shoot me! Shoot me! I can't show up at the party in jeans and a t-shirt. Lola Franklin is going to be there."

Peter holstered his gun. "Help me out here, Piper. Who's Lola Franklin?"

"Lola Franklin is a YouTube star, who starred on the television show *What's Eating Johnny?* She was married to the twelfth richest man in America and divorced him in a contentious court battle that netted her fifty million dollars," Piper said.

"Wow, you never cease to amaze me with your knowledge of trivia," Peter said, honestly impressed.

"Oh, Adesh told me all about it. That's how I know," Piper said. "Adesh is in love with Lola."

"And I *was* going to marry her, but now I can't because of the suit," Adesh moaned. He threw himself down on a chair and put his head in his hands.

"I know how to sew," Piper said.

"You can?" Peter asked.

She seemed to think about it for a moment. "Yes. I know how to sew, and I can let out the suit so Adesh can wear it."

Peter kissed her lightly on the cheek. "You're an amazing woman."

"Not that amazing. No one's trying to kill me. Hey, maybe some will try to kill me at the party," she said, hopefully. "It's going to be full of big shots, right?"

Peter nodded. "I don't know why we got invited. It's way too high class for us."

"Maybe we got invited because I'm filthy rich," Piper suggested.

"Maybe," Peter said. "One thing's for sure, though, watching baseball on TV while eating a sub sandwich would be a lot more exciting than a hoity-toity party."

CHAPTER 2

The funny thing about having amnesia was that everything was a new experience for Piper. She knew how to brush her teeth and read, but she didn't remember ever doing it before she ran naked and terrified through the redwood forest a few weeks before.

So, when Peter, Adesh, and she walked into the San Francisco Gemology Museum, it was all new to her. Had she ever gone to a museum before? She didn't have a clue. Had she ever gone to a fancy party in a museum before? She had even less of a clue.

The museum sat on a tall hill in the city with an incredible view of the Golden Gate Bridge and Alcatraz. They were met at the entrance by a woman in an evening gown, and Peter handed her their invitations. She felt him put his hand on the small of her back, and they walked in.

The museum was completely lit by candlelight, and two harpists played in a corner by a display of giant rubies.

"I see the shrimp puff guy. I'm going to head them off," Adesh said. "But if you see Lola, give me a heads up so I can get rid of the shrimp in time. I want her to think of me as a vegan and totally wrapped up in my physique."

"No problem, buddy," Peter told him. "Your vegan physique is safe with me."

Adesh walked toward a caterer who held a platter of shrimp puffs, while Peter and Piper took a tour of the periphery of the main room. Every few feet, there was a glass enclosure set into the wall with an amazing jewel inside.

"*Hat Clasp*," Piper read on a gold plaque next to one of the windows. "Sixteen carat diamond on it. That seems excessive for a hat."

"How about diamonds? You like diamonds?" Peter asked.

"They're all right."

"How about rubies? Emeralds? What's your favorite gem?"

The hair on the back of Piper's neck stood up,

and she felt Peter's eyes on her, like she was a gazelle at the watering hole and he was a hungry lion, trying to figure out which way she was going to run so that he wouldn't miss out on dinner.

She turned away from the hat clasp and met Peter's eyes. Gone was the hyper self-assured superspy, and in his place was a little boy, waiting for an answer.

But what was the question?

"Why are you so curious about what gems I like?" she asked him.

He stuffed his hands into his pockets and looked down at his shoes. "No reason."

"Gems are nice, but I'm not a jewelry girl," she said honestly. Her hand found the key around her neck, and she clasped it. It wasn't jewelry, but it was her only true possession besides a debit card, and she didn't know what it unlocked.

"Oh," Peter said, obviously disappointed with her answer.

Piper stepped forward until she could smell Peter's aftershave. She grabbed his lapels and pulled him in close. Resting her cheek on his broad, hard chest, she took a moment to breathe him in.

"Just because I don't want a rock on my finger doesn't mean I don't want a rock on my finger. You know what I mean?" she said.

"Sort of. But…"

Suddenly, the moment was over, and Piper pushed away from him with force. "Oh my gosh. That's Lola Franklin, and she's heading in Adesh's direction."

Peter turned around and followed Piper's gaze to Lola Franklin. They watched as she, who was decked out in a sequined strapless gown and enormous silicone breasts, sauntered over to the shrimp puffs waiter. Adesh had his back to her, so he wasn't aware that he was about to be found out as a shrimp puff eater and totally unconcerned about his physique or about being vegan.

Adesh's coat had come undone with his hands' swift movements as they swept one shrimp puff after another off the tray and into his mouth.

"Help him," Piper urged Peter.

"Help him? I don't like shrimp puffs. They back up on me. Now, if there was a sub sandwich, I would be all over that."

Piper punched Peter in the arm. "No, not the shrimp puffs. Stop him before Lola sees him. Or distract Lola. Do something. Help your best friend."

"Best friend? I wouldn't go that far. I have a lot of friends."

"Oh, yeah?" Piper asked. "Your last friend tried to kill us. You don't know who your friends are. But Adesh is definitely a friend."

Peter squinted at her. "Oh, I get it. So, you're deciding who my best friend is for me."

"Do you have a problem with that?"

Peter smiled. "Not at all. I trust your judgment. Presto chango, Adesh is now my best friend."

Piper gave him a little nudge. "Good. Go help your best friend."

Peter untied one of his shoes and practically skipped to Lola. When he got to her, he pretended to trip over his shoelace and crashed into her. "Sorry about that, *Lola Franklin!*" he bellowed. "I didn't see you there, *Lola Franklin!*"

Adesh started and choked on a shrimp puff. He whipped around and his eyes found Lola. In shock, he stumbled to the side, knocking the shrimp puff platter up in the air. It flew until it hit the display of rubies. To Adesh's credit, he regained his composure quickly and buttoned his jacket. He slipped a pained smile on his face and stepped toward Lola and Peter.

"So sorry," Peter told Lola, who didn't look pleased. "May I introduce you to my best friend?" he asked her and winked at Piper. "Adesh Sharma is one of America's preeminent information technology barons. Adesh, this is Lola Franklin. She's an actress."

Smooth. Like a new jar of peanut butter.

If Lola wasn't interested in a four-hundred-pound hacker, she was sure interested in one of America's preeminent information technology barons. Her eyes seemed to grow twice their normal size, and Piper could practically hear her brain shout *jackpot!* Piper guessed that Lola had set her sights on more than a fifty-million-dollar settlement.

She put her hand out to Adesh, and he brought it to his lips and kissed it.

"Uh…" he stammered. "Um… Uh… Um…"

Peter rolled his eyes at Piper, and she gestured back at him to help Adesh.

"Did you see the sword with seven hundred and seventy diamonds on the hilt? I'm sure Adesh would show it to you," Peter told Lola.

"I would like that," Lola gushed in a breathy Marilyn Monroe voice.

Peter stepped back out of their way. Adesh stared at Lola without blinking. Piper worried that he was having a stroke, and she tried to think of how to save a stroke victim, but for once, she couldn't bring up the details.

Luckily, Adesh finally blinked. Then, he smiled and took Lola's hand and led her toward the sword display.

Peter blew on his knuckles and rubbed them on his shirt, while he smiled at Piper and walked to her. "Not bad, right?"

"I'm impressed."

"Finally. If I knew that fixing up Adesh was all it took to impress you, I would have done it long ago."

"You've impressed me in other ways," she said and felt herself blush.

Peter smirked at her, and she knew that look instantly. The sex look. She gnawed on the inside of her cheek thinking about it.

"I've never had sex in a gem museum," she said. "At least I don't think I have."

Peter arched an eyebrow and smirked. "Odds are pretty good you've never had sex in a gem museum, but the odds are pretty good that we can change that."

Piper felt herself warm up, and her mouth went dry. She put her hands on her hips. "Here? This is a high class, upscale, black tie event. This is a museum. Shouldn't we have respect for a museum? For academia? For science and charity? For culture."

Peter looked up at the ceiling, as if he was thinking about it. "I'm guessing no."

"I agree. Let's go," she said and grabbed his hand.

"Where are we going to do it?"

Piper scanned the area. Rich people were mixing and mingling, drinking profusely and pretending to eat. The harpists continued to play in the dim candlelight.

Rich people were all sucking in their stomachs as they got thoroughly sauced.

Then, she saw the perfect place for Peter and her to do the dirty deed. A big sign at the end of the room announced the *Royal White Diamond. 49-Carats of Beauty and Wonder.*

Piper pointed to the sign.

"Forty-nine carats of beauty and wonder," Peter mused. "Sounds like a particular part of my anatomy that you're very familiar with."

Piper elbowed him in the side. "Don't break the moment with talk of your anatomy. Any more frat boy behavior, and I'll turn around and go for the shrimp puffs instead," she lied.

"My lips are sealed unless you want some lip action. I'm all for the lip action."

They followed the sign to a small room, which was dedicated entirely to the ginormous Royal White Diamond. It was lit with candlelight in here, too. The walls were decked out in signs about the history of the diamond and its importance and value. In the center of the room was a glass dome on top of a pedestal. Piper squinted in the dim light to see the diamond under the glass. Normally, it must have been lit dramatically, but now it was just a huge rock in candlelight.

As soon as they walked into the room, Peter

stepped behind her and wrapped his arms around her waist, pulling her back close to him so that she could feel every hard inch of him.

Her head fell back onto his chest, as her body grew hot and her core melted and throbbed. Peter stepped forward, moving her while he walked toward the glass dome.

They were going to have sex on the diamond dome! That was one for the record books, Piper thought. She made a mental note to get a notebook and keep track of the places they had sex. It would be like X-rated scrapbooking.

They took another couple steps, and Piper's foot knocked into something hard. A shockwave of pain went through her, and there was an audible clang when her foot made contact with the object.

"What the hell?" Peter asked. He let go of Piper and stepped around her. There was another clang, and Peter yelped and hopped around for a moment. He recovered quickly and pulled his phone out of his pocket and shined the light on the floor.

"It's an axe," Peter said.

"It's a single bit, felling axe with a long, hickory handle," Piper said.

"There's blood on the blade."

"There's blood on the blade," Piper repeated.

"Blood?"

Peter stood up straight and shined the light in Piper's face. "What did you do?"

"Me? Nothing. It's not me this time. That blood has nothing to do with me." She gnawed on her lower lip. "At least, I don't think it does."

Peter lowered the light and scanned the room with it. There, sticking out from behind the diamond's pedestal was an arm.

"It's an arm," Piper said.

"It's an arm with blood on it," Peter said.

They walked toward it to get a better look. A very small man dressed in black was lying dead and bloody on the floor. He had been wearing a black ski mask, but it had been pulled off, revealing his face. There was a lot of blood on the man and around him.

Peter pointed at him. "I think the axe was his."

"Why?"

"I think he was using it to steal the diamond." Peter went back to the entrance and she watched as he flipped on the light switch. Nothing happened. No light. "He must have cut off the electricity, but no one noticed because the museum is being lit with candles for the party."

Piper stomped her foot on the floor. "I can't believe someone was murdered and no one tried to kill me."

"You must be losing your mojo."

Piper stayed with the body while Peter left to alert the museum about the electricity and the dead body. A couple minutes later, the lights came on, and a minute after that, Peter returned with two security guards and the woman who had greeted them at the door.

She took one look at the dead body and screamed. One of the security guards held onto his stomach, as if he was going to be sick.

"I didn't do it," Piper said.

"What she means is that we discovered the body," Peter corrected.

"No one tried to kill me," she explained.

"Not like anyone would want to," Peter supplied. "Obviously, the man was trying to steal the diamond and was murdered. Maybe his partner did it."

"Maybe it was self-inflicted," one of the security guards suggested.

Peter shook his head slowly. "No. It wasn't self-inflicted. He was axed in the back. He couldn't have done that to himself."

"He might have. Some folks are very limber," the guard countered.

"No. Nobody's that limber," Peter insisted, gently. "Arms only bend in one direction."

There was noise outside the room, and a few people entered, including Adesh and Lola. Adesh's mouth dropped open, and he wagged his finger at Piper. "What did you do?"

"It wasn't me. Nobody tried to kill me," she insisted.

"As if," Adesh said.

CHAPTER 3

Peter was down in the dumps. It had been three days since Piper and he had discovered the dead body in the museum. Local law enforcement had questioned them briefly but refused any of Peter's theories of what had happened and who the murderer could be.

Not that Peter knew who the murderer could be, but he was surprised to find himself ready to find out. Piper was interested in finding out, too, but she wasn't feeling like the has-been, used-to-be-needed, retirement-is-death, ex-super-spies-get-no-love feeling he was feeling.

Peter had tried to point out certain aspects of the crime to the police on the scene, but he was ushered out, just like he was a suburban dad who had recently binge-watched a Netflix thriller series and was about to corrupt a crime scene with dirty fingers.

"I'm not a suburban dad," Peter said aloud. His voice came out like the moper that he had become, and he chomped down on his lip so he wouldn't betray more of his pathetic mindset.

"You're not a dad," Adesh said. He had been hunched over his computer for hours, working with Peter to figure out who had called Peter weeks ago, urging him to go to the redwood forest in the middle of the night where he met Piper. Since they had been trying to solve the mystery of Piper's past, Peter believed it was essential to track down that caller to give Piper back her memories.

Adesh looked up from the monitor. "Are you a dad?" he asked Peter.

"No. Focus, Adesh."

Adesh scratched his chin. "I did think Piper was looking a little puffy lately."

"Piper isn't pregnant. I'm not going to be a dad. At least not now. Not for a long time."

"It's probably not a good idea to have a baby while folks are trying to kill you," Adesh said, cocking his head to the side, as if he was contemplating the radius of the earth.

"And if she's puffy, and I'm not saying she is," Peter said. "It's because we ate nachos for dinner last night."

"Although, no one's tried to kill you for a few weeks, so maybe that's over," Adesh continued. "You know, like a cold. That usually lasts ten to fourteen days. But then you can get another cold. Or the cold can go into your sinuses or your chest. My aunt died that way. She got a cold that turned into pancreatic cancer, and she died like that." Adesh snapped his fingers to illustrate how fast his aunt's cold killed her.

Peter grabbed one of Adesh's Pop-Tarts and took a bite. "I'm almost a hundred percent sure that a cold can't turn into pancreatic cancer," he said.

"Think about it. It's like the Transformers. One minute they're killer alien robots, and the next minute they're an American-made car."

Peter pointed at him. "You have a point. I take it all back."

"So, Piper's pregnant?" Adesh asked, leaning forward. "I thought she was looking puffy."

"Nachos. No. Not pregnant. I'm not a dad."

Adesh slapped his desk and smiled wide. "I get it! You're worried that you're *like* a suburban dad. Yeah, you sort of are."

Peter gulped in air and choked on the Pop-Tart. "No, I'm not," he said, when his throat finally cleared. "I'm not suburban, and I'm not a dad."

"You're wearing cotton Dockers."

"These aren't Dockers. These are Urban Comfort Slacks from Saks Fifth Avenue."

Adesh shook his head. "They look just like cotton Dockers to me."

"And I don't live in the suburbs. This house is in the heart of the city of San Francisco."

"There's an Instant Pot in the kitchen. That sort of says suburbs, you know. Anything except for a wok and takeout is suburbs in the kitchen."

Peter put his hand up, palm forward. "Let's end this conversation. It's getting ugly. Let's agree that I'm not a suburban dad."

"I'm agreeing because I know you have a gun strapped to your ankle," Adesh said.

"I've got two guns on my body and three knives. Smart man."

Adesh was probably the best hacker on the planet. For whatever reason, he had decided to work exclusively for Peter and live with him and Piper. They had become a little family, but Peter secretly worried that Adesh would get bored and hack into every country's defense system and start World War Three.

Adesh turned his attention back to his monitor. "This man's a ghost," Adesh said and leaned back in his chair. "He left no fingerprints or footprints or even a snail trail. He's a ghost."

"So, it's hopeless?" Peter asked. It was hard to believe. If Adesh couldn't find the caller, he was unfindable.

Adesh's face dropped, like he had just been informed that the mayor of San Francisco had made processed foods illegal. "Do you think I can't do it?" Adesh croaked, his voice filled with emotion. "You think I can't find the caller?"

That was exactly what Peter thought. They had been looking for him for weeks, and now that they had a Pentagon-level computer set-up in the house, and Adesh still couldn't find the caller, Peter believed down to his soul that it was hopeless. They couldn't find the caller. Their last clue had evaporated, and they probably would never find out who Piper was.

But Adesh was looking at him, as if Peter's response was the key to Adesh's emotional and psychological health. Peter had killed people in the name of his country, but he couldn't let down a friend.

Especially not a friend who was looking at him like he hung the moon and his approval was the key to his happiness.

Peter smiled wide and patted Adesh's back. "Of course I think you can do it. Think? Know! I know you can do it. You're the number one hacker on the planet.

Whoever the caller was, he has nothing on your skills. You got mad skills, bro. Mad skills. You're the LeBron James of keyboards. You're the Tom Brady of software."

Adesh's face brightened. "I like Tom Brady. His wife is hot."

Peter elbowed him. "Not as hot as Lola Franklin, am I right?"

"She told me that she would go to Comic Con with me, maybe," Adesh said, blushing. "That was before the dead body, though, so I didn't get her contact information."

"But you found her contact information since then, I'm guessing."

Adesh showed Peter his phone. "Found and made her a new contact. I'm going to text her once I figure out my cosplay for Comic Con so I can offer her a costume to go with mine. I think she'll like it."

"I'm sure she will," Peter lied. "All right. I'm going to let you continue with your super-hacking. I have to check on Piper and see if she's in the mood to get naked."

Peter left the office and climbed the stairs to the main floor. The new house was about five thousand square feet on four floors. He found Piper in the kitchen, taking the dishwasher apart.

"Another one?" Peter asked. For some reason, she

was more or less obsessed with household appliances since they moved in, and she had already taken apart the microwave and the George Foreman grill.

Piper looked up at him from her place sitting cross-legged on the floor with a screwdriver in one hand. She blew a strand of her long red hair off her face. "I'm sorry, but it's amazing. It washes dishes!"

"Yes, I know. My mother made me load the dishwasher every day for years. My brother Spencer was in charge of emptying it."

"And it dries them, too," Piper said, excitedly. "Did you know that?"

"Yes. I'm surprised you didn't. You know everything." Peter's phone rang, and he looked at the screen. "Holy shit. It's the former bosses. What do they want?"

"Maybe they want you to save the world," Piper suggested with more than a little hope in her voice.

"I'm retired."

"Okay," she said, sounding disappointed.

"I'll take the call in my office," he said and left the kitchen.

Peter had a small office down the hall from the master bedroom. It was nowhere near the size of Adesh's office, but it had a small desk, a laptop, and a large safe with enough weaponry to overthrow a medium-sized country.

He sat at his desk and touched a button in one of the drawers. The top of the desk opened, and a screen rose. It turned on, and Peter's former boss, flanked by two four-star generals, appeared.

"Good morning, Peter," his former boss said.

"Yep," Peter replied.

"We need you for one last mission."

Peter leaned back in his chair and put his feet on the desk, crossing them at the ankle. "I already did my last mission. I'm retired."

"Your country is calling on you, young man," one of the generals growled.

"Young man? Thanks, Dad, but no thanks," Peter said and studied his fingernails for effect.

"Peter," his former boss said, his voice steel. "It's an easy one. An important one."

"Look, I'm busy," Peter said. "I have important things to do, like have sex with my girlfriend and figure out new ways to spend her money."

And figure out who she is and why half of the world wants her dead, he thought, but he decided to keep that to himself.

"This is the great superspy you spoke about? This guy?" the other general demanded, pointing at Peter.

"Listen, Peter," his former boss said, ignoring the

general. "We registered a huge spike of nuclear isotopes in Russia."

Peter laid his hands in his lap. "You got my attention."

"Russia hasn't put out a statement. They're not talking, and we're not telling them we know about it."

That made sense. The country wouldn't want to divulge their intelligence capabilities to Russia.

"This is an easy one," Peter's boss continued. "Fast. You can take your girlfriend, too. That would be good for your cover. It would make you look less suspicious. Find out about the nuclear isotopes."

"I'm retired," Peter insisted a little too quickly. He felt he had to reject the offer fast before he became too intrigued and accepted another mission. He was retired, and he was involved with Piper. He had other things to do. His life as a spy was behind him.

"What nuclear isotopes?" Peter heard from behind him. He turned around. Piper still had a screwdriver in her hand, and she was craning her head to see the monitor. "What do you mean I can go, too? Where? Where?"

Peter muted the call. "I'm retired," he told Piper.

"You could do a little retirement pause," she suggested excitedly. "We could investigate the nuclear isotopes together, and then you can retire immediately after. Where are the nuclear isotopes?"

"Russia, but we have other things to do. Remember, you don't know who you are."

Piper touched the key that hung around her neck. "I've never been to Russia. At least, I don't think I have. Russia sounds nice."

"But…"

"Please. Please, please, please. Oh, please."

Peter's body warmed. He was head over heels in love with Piper, and when she begged, he turned to mush.

CHAPTER 4

After they said their goodbyes to Adesh, they hopped onto a private plane on their way to St. Petersburg. The government was giving them a first-class stipend to pose as a rich couple on a vacation, but the government's idea of a first-class stipend didn't compete with Piper's bank account.

So, they rejected the offer of an economy seat on a Russian airline and took a private plane to St. Petersburg. When they landed, they were met by two Russian hulks in a large black SUV.

Their black suits bulged with muscles and what Piper assumed were guns in shoulder holsters. They were more muscular than Peter, but Peter towered over them in his large, six-foot-six frame.

Peter nodded at them and opened the back seat door for Piper. She slipped inside, and he sat next to her. As soon as the driver started the car, the hulk in the passenger seat turned around and passed Peter a gun.

Peter waved him off. "I've got my own."

"Government-issued?" the hulk asked him.

"No."

"Lucky," the hulk complained.

They drove to a hotel with no name. It turned out that the richest of the rich in Russia stayed at the no-name hotel. Piper waited outside in front of the hotel while Peter said a few last things to the two hulks and handled the luggage.

Rich, well-dressed people came and went from the hotel, and Piper enjoyed watching them, like she was at a fashion show. Suddenly, there was a loud screech of a car's brakes and then a loud crash as a white Lamborghini slammed into a small Toyota, crushing the back of it like an accordion.

A man stumbled out of the Toyota and clutched his bloody forehead, where he must have hit it on the steering wheel. He looked down at his car in a state of shock. A long, lanky woman stepped out of the Lamborghini. She was wearing four-inch heels and a white, designer sheath dress, along with enough gold jewelry to weigh down a large man. Her hair was perfectly coiffed, and her face was covered in a few, thick layers of makeup.

Her eyes found the injured man, and her face turned down in what could only be described as fury. She wagged her finger at him. It had a long pointy fingernail, which was painted white.

"How dare you get in my way!" she screamed at him. Since she had been the one who crashed into him, not the other way around, it was outlandish that she was attacking him.

"Why are you even driving on this road with that crappy, old, cheap car?" she shrieked at him. "And your clothes! Shabby, shabby clothes! How dare you get in my way!"

Peter joined Piper in front of the hotel and wrapped his arm around her waist. "Watching from the sidelines? That's new for us," he said.

"Can you believe what she's saying?" Piper asked him.

The woman was still haranguing the injured man, insulting his car and his clothes. Luckily, Piper heard a police siren on its way, and she hoped the Lamborghini driver was going to be arrested.

"I can't believe what she's saying," Peter said. "Of course, I don't understand Russian, so maybe that's why I don't believe it."

"But she's speaking English," Piper said.

"I was a bad student, but I wasn't that bad. I know English when I hear it, and that ain't it."

At first, Piper thought that Peter was playing a trick on her, but as she continued to listen to the woman yell, she realized he was right. It wasn't English.

Piper gasped. She turned to face Peter and clutched his shoulders in excitement. "It's Russian!" she exclaimed.

"Makes sense since we're in Russia."

"I can understand Russian. I understand every word. This is a clue, Peter. A clue! You know what this means?"

Peter shook his head. "No, but I'm hoping it means you're a Russian princess with even more money and a castle or two."

"No, it doesn't mean that," Piper said. "It means I'm probably an interpreter for the United Nations."

Peter's face dropped. "That's not as good as a princess, but I'll take it. Shall we check in?"

They entered the hotel with no name. The lobby practically dripped with gold. Everything was coated in it. It didn't look like a hotel lobby. There was no check-in desk or a concierge. Instead, the moment they entered, they were surrounded by staff who somehow knew who they were and gave them their key, took their luggage, and offered them spa and food services.

But they didn't show them to their room because Peter and Piper were supposed to go on a tour. "We are?" Piper asked, surprised. They were only posing as tourists, but maybe it was part of the plan.

Peter shrugged. "Beats me."

A tour guide approached them. She was middle-aged with a platinum blonde bouffant hairdo. She was wearing a tight blue Chanel suit and high heels. Her lips were painted with deep red lipstick, which had run into the small lines that surrounded her mouth. Blue eyeshadow covered her eyelids, and black mascara hung off her eyelashes in clumps.

"I'm underdressed for Russia, I think," Piper whispered to Peter. She was wearing jeans and a white peasant blouse, flat sneakers, and a hippy bag draped over her shoulder.

Peter put his hand on her ass and gave it a squeeze. "I love when you say *underdressed*. It gets me hot."

Piper felt her insides melt into a mound of estrogen jelly. "You're always hot," she whispered back and giggled.

"I am Irina, your tour guide," the tour guide told them. "Your first-class luxury tour is about to start. Please," she said, gesturing with her hand toward the door.

Peter and Piper left the hotel with her. They were surprised to find a tour bus waiting for them outside. It definitely didn't look like first-class luxury, but Piper wondered if it was all a ruse organized by the U.S. government to get them closer to discovering more about the nuclear isotope spike.

"After you, beautiful," Peter told Piper. She climbed on board. There were about ten other people on the bus in addition to the bus driver, who was reading a newspaper.

Peter and Piper sat in the seats behind the driver. Irina told the bus driver to start the bus, and she stood at the front of the bus and talked into a microphone.

"Today we are seeing the greatest cultural achievements on the planet," she announced, gravely, as if she was daring everyone to deny that St. Petersburg held the greatest achievements on the planet.

The bus drove through town, as Irina continued to talk into the microphone. "To our left is the neever reever. Peter the Great sailed down the neever reever. So did Catherine the Great. She very much like the neever reever."

"What the hell is the neever reever?" Peter asked Piper.

"I think she's saying Neva River. It was of

enormous strategic importance to Russia, Sweden, and Finland. Peter the Great was very protective over it."

"And now, we will stop and admire the neever reever," Irina said, and the bus parked on a picturesque bridge over the river where other tourists were leaning against a short stone wall and taking selfies.

Peter and Piper waited for the passengers to exit before them so that Peter could scope out the others and surreptitiously take photos of them with his superspy watch.

The tour group was a motley crew from every spectrum of society. There was an elderly couple, who were oozing money. There was a young family with four kids, and there were three college-age young adults, who were partying hard all the way through Irina's speech.

The two college-aged guys and one girl were each holding a bottle of vodka as they filed past Peter and Piper on their way off the bus. "I'm telling you that Russian vodka is easy to drink, as long as you eat bread first," one of them said with confidence. "Look at me. Two shots and I'm completely fine."

Peter rolled his eyes at Piper. "I think I've seen this movie before," he told her.

Outside, Peter wrapped his arm around Piper's waist, as they admired the Neva River. St. Petersburg was a beautiful place with historic and impressive monuments. Piper was grateful to see it with Peter.

"I can see what Peter the Great saw in the neever reever," Peter said. "As reevers go, it's aces."

Next to them, the young people were going at the vodka bottles like they were energy drinks. After a few minutes, Irina announced that it was time to continue the tour.

"But you cannot go back in the bus," she told the drunk young people. "You'll throw up when the bus moves."

"I'm not dunk," one of them insisted. His vodka bottle slipped out of his hand and crashed onto the ground, breaking into a million pieces. "I'm potally fine."

Irina shook her finger at him. She was furious and would brook no argument. "No. You're drunk like all Americans, and you will vomit in the bus when it runs. You cannot go back on the bus."

"I'm not…" the man started but belched instead and then seemed to forget his train of thought.

"I can't look away," Peter told Piper. "It's like a train wreck. I'm riveted. I feel guilty about it, but there's no stopping it."

"We're going on the bus," the girl shrieked at Irina. "Bus! Bus! Bus!" Her face was bright red, and her skin was blotchy from the alcohol.

Irina threw up her hands. "Fine. But you have to

vomit now before you get on the bus. Throw up into the neever reever."

"This is getting good," Peter said to Piper. "I think Hollywood calls this a plot twist."

The three looked doubtful, but with Irina's persistence, they all bent over the wall and tried to vomit into the river.

"I'm guessing that Peter the Great wouldn't approve," Peter said to Piper.

One of the men and the girl were successful, but the other guy couldn't throw up, no matter how hard he tried.

"See? I'm not shick," he told Irina.

"No bus," she told him. "No bus until you throw up." She turned toward his friends. "Punch him in the stomach. Then, he will throw up."

"I wish I had popcorn," Peter told Piper. "This would be even better with popcorn."

"What did she say?" the girl asked her friend as she wiped her mouth.

"She said to punch Joe in the stomach so he'll upchuck," her friend answered.

"Okay," she said and punched her friend Joe in the stomach.

"You can't make this shit up," Peter said to Piper.

"I'm not sure what's happening," Piper replied.

"It doesn't matter," Peter said. "It's like the last *Mission Impossible* movie. We don't need to understand the plot. We just need to sit back and enjoy it. Damn, I wish I had some popcorn."

Joe's friends took turns punching him in the stomach but to no avail.

"I guess Joe isn't a puker," Peter said to Piper. "Ah, well. We can't all be perfect."

After some pleading with Irina from the young group, she finally relented. Joe was not going to vomit, it was determined. So, they all filed back onto the bus.

"Now, we are going to the Hermitage Museum, the greatest museum in the world," Irina announced with her microphone. "Some say the Louvre is the greatest, but that is a big joke. Big joke. Big! Ha!" she said. "Start the bus, you lazy ass," she told the driver.

Peter held Piper's hand and gave it a squeeze. "This is so good," he said, obviously thrilled with the bizarre tour.

They sat in front again, right behind the bus driver with Peter by the window and Piper on the aisle. Two of the drunk people were sitting directly behind them, and Joe was relegated to isolation in his own seat across the aisle from Peter and Piper.

"Here we go," Peter whispered to Piper. "It's like Space Mountain in Disneyland."

"I wonder if I've ever been to Disneyland," she said.

The bus driver put down his newspaper and started the bus. As soon as the motor started and he put it into gear, the girl behind Piper moaned and then violently threw up.

The vomit spewed through the air like a power washer. At least that's what Piper thought it looked like. Her head was turned away from it, but it sounded just like a power washer. And when it hit the top of Piper's head, it landed with such force that she was pushed forward, letting it drip down her face.

"I feel much better," the girl behind Piper announced.

"Keep driving," Irina growled at the bus driver. "We must get to the Hermitage."

Peter took a handkerchief out of his pocket and wiped Piper's face. "I'm trying not to laugh because I love you, and I want you to keep sleeping with me," he said.

Piper's eyes were closed in order not to get vomit in her eyes, but she cracked one open slightly to see Peter's smirk.

"You're laughing at me," Piper said, when her mouth had been wiped clean.

"I swear I'm not laughing," he said.

"You're laughing, but I understand. That was the

grossest thing I've ever experienced. Ever."

"Totally gross," Peter agreed.

"The good thing is that will probably be the grossest thing that ever happens to me," she said, trying to be optimistic.

"You shouldn't have said that. You'll give yourself the evil eye," Peter warned.

The bus turned left, and as if on cue, Joe moaned across the aisle.

Uh-oh.

"Don't you do it!" Piper yelled at him.

He moaned, again.

"Don't you dare!" she shouted.

"Here you go." Peter handed Piper a t-shirt and sweatpants that he had bought in the Hermitage Museum's gift shop. He was wearing a new t-shirt, too because he had given her the shirt off his back in the bus in order to clean herself up after Joe threw up all over her.

"He must have eaten a really big breakfast," Piper noted, taking the clothes from Peter. They were standing just outside the women's bathroom. The rest of the tour group had gone into the museum to see its wonders, but Piper was impatient to wash herself as best as she could in the bathroom sink.

"It must have been a buffet," Peter agreed. "There's chunks of home fried potatoes in your hair." He leaned down and inspected the top of her head. "Nope. Not home fried potatoes. I think that's a ham omelet."

"It was the grossest thing I've ever seen," Piper said, reliving the horrible moment. "He opened his mouth, and I actually saw the vomit shoot up his throat, and then it was all over me."

Peter nodded. "It was incredible aim, like a professional baseball pitcher or something. But, you know, with vomit instead of a baseball."

"It shot up and paused midstream for a split second, as if it was deciding whether to hit me or not," Piper continued. "And then it just went for it. *Pow!* It went on forever, like a dam bursting."

"I know. I witnessed the whole thing. Impressive. And crazy how none of it got on me."

Piper narrowed her eyes at him. "Shut up, or I'll rub my ham omelet hair on your new t-shirt."

She opened the bathroom door and walked inside. Luckily, she was the only one in the bathroom. Catching her reflection in one of the mirrors, she gasped. It was worse than she expected.

She leaned forward to get a better look. "That's not a ham omelet," she said, studying her hair. "That's home fried potatoes, for sure."

Since Piper had already been abducted, tortured, and almost murdered several times, she didn't allow herself to feel sorry for herself just because she had gotten thrown up on twice today.

She placed the gift shop clothes on a nearby sink and turned the water on in another. She took her pants and shirt off and tossed them into a trashcan. She ducked her head under the tap in order to get rid of Joe's breakfast.

After a couple of minutes of washing her hair with water and soap from the dispenser, she heard the door to the bathroom open, and she turned her head slightly to see Irina come in.

"Sorry for the undress. Just trying to get clean," Piper said.

"Don't bother," Irina said and pulled out a switchblade from her bag. She pointed it at Piper and sneered at her with menace.

Oh, no, Piper thought. *Someone is going to try and kill me in a bathroom. Again.*

CHAPTER 5

Peter stood outside the bathroom and waited for Piper to clean herself up. He was supposed to be focused on Russian nuclear isotopes, but he was focused on Piper and their future together instead.

Specifically, he was thinking about her dislike of gems and jewelry. She had told him that if even if she didn't want a rock on her finger, that didn't mean she didn't want a rock on her finger.

What did that mean?

And how could he propose without a ring?

He wanted to propose. He wanted to lock Piper down before she realized that she was too good for him. He wanted to know that he was going to wake up to her every morning. He wanted to grow old with her and have lots of little Pipers crawling around, calling him Daddy.

Yikes. When did I become so sappy?

Irina walked down the hall toward him. He waved at her, and she waved back before she opened the door and walked into the bathroom.

"Piper, I've been thinking about us and the ring," Peter called out, hoping his voice carried through the closed door. He didn't care if Irina could hear or not because he wasn't shy about letting his feelings for Piper known to the world.

"You know I'm crazy about you," he continued to the door. "Sure, you've almost got me killed more times than I can count, but I still love you."

There was a grunt of complaint from inside the bathroom.

Uh-oh. Peter better ramp up the romance talk and avoid mentioning that Piper was a lot of trouble.

"I don't mean that you're a lot of trouble," he continued in his most sultry voice. "I mean that you're dangerous, and that's exciting."

There was another loud grunt, and a loud noise, as if Piper had hit the sink in anger. *Get it together, Bolton. This is a proposal, not a job review.*

"I mean, I love you, and I want to spend my life with you," he said. There was a loud crash from inside the bathroom, and then a scream. "I know that scream,"

Peter said. "That's the scream of the woman I love and want to spend my life with."

She screamed again, and it was echoed by another scream. The second scream sounded like a cat in heat.

A very angry cat in heat.

Peter rolled his eyes and sighed. He opened the bathroom door.

Inside, he saw Irina attacking Piper with a knife in her hand. Piper was wearing only a bra and panties, and she was soaking wet while she was battling Irina. It was a scene straight out of one of Peter's fantasies, but he had to remind himself that Piper's life was in danger and it wasn't the time to admire his half-naked, wet woman.

Irina's arm was outstretched in an effort to stab Piper, but Piper had blocked her arm with her own. Irina growled like a villain in a James Bond movie.

"Help! Killer! Help!" Piper squeaked.

"I can't believe this is happening in a bathroom again," Peter complained. He had already saved her once in a bathroom, and now she needed to be saved again.

"Now's not the time for a conversation," Piper urged.

"Right," he said and launched himself at Irina.

The Russian tour guide was a small, thin woman, and Peter was sure that it would be no trouble to subdue her, but when he got close, Irina rounded on him and sliced through his new t-shirt with her knife.

Peter jumped back out of arm's reach.

"What did you do to her?" Peter demanded at Piper.

"Nothing! She came in and tried to kill me."

"Maybe you said something insulting in Russian."

"I might have said hello," Piper said, thinking about it.

Irina launched herself at Peter, and he was shocked as hell to find himself on the floor. "She's a wily one," he said.

"Get her! Get her!" Piper yelled.

"I'm trying," he said, trying to maneuver around Irina's knife. "She knows some kind of martial art that I'm not familiar with."

Irina spat something horrible at him in Russian.

"What did she say?" Peter asked Piper, while he managed to stand.

"She said you're a capitalist pig, and you'll have to die for the motherland," Piper replied.

"This really is a James Bond movie," Peter said. "A good one starring Sean Connery."

But Peter had had enough. He wasn't going to be murdered by a skinny woman in bad makeup. Maybe another day, but not today. He front-kicked Irina in the knee, and she went down like a ton of bricks. The knife flew out of her hand and hit one of the sinks. She started to get up to attack him again, but Peter pointed at her and shook his head.

"If you get up, I'll punch you in the face. Repeatedly. Lots and lots of times," he warned.

She sat back on the floor. Piper asked her something in Russian, and Irina shook her head violently. Then, Piper asked her something else, and Irina clamped her mouth closed so hard that her lips disappeared.

"She won't talk," Piper said.

"She doesn't have to," Peter said. "Her knife is FSB issued. She's Russian Intelligence Service."

Peter turned his head for a second to point out the knife to Piper. When he turned back around, Irina was bringing a small capsule toward her mouth. Peter leapt toward her and slapped her hand, making her drop the capsule.

"Cyanide capsule?" he asked, incredulous. "That's pretty old school, Irina. What's so important that you would rather commit suicide than talk to us?"

But he knew of course. It was all about the spike in nuclear isotopes.

Peter leaned back against a sink and tapped his chin with his index finger. "The thing I don't get is why you went after Piper and not me," he said.

Irina smiled. "Take care of the weak one first. Simple," she decided to answer.

The bathroom door opened, and three men ran in, each with a gun raised. Peter's body tensed, ready to fight, but almost immediately, he recognized them for who they were. American military. There was no hiding their posture and the way they moved.

Peter raised his hands, and Piper followed.

Two of the men secured Irina and gave her an injection in the arm. Another man entered, wearing a paramedic uniform and pushing a stretcher. Irina's eyes closed a second after the shot was administered. The men lifted her unconscious body onto the stretcher and covered her with a blanket.

"You sure make a lot of noise," one of the men said to Peter.

Peter pointed at Piper. "Don't look at me. It was her fault."

"I was just washing myself, and she tried to kill me," Piper insisted.

The man looked her up and down. She was still wet and wearing only her bra and panties. She had the hottest body that Peter had had ever seen, and he was sure that her effect was not lost on the military operative. Peter stepped forward. "No," he told the man. "Just no."

"Sorry, bro," he replied.

Irina was carried out of the bathroom, and the three men escorted Peter and Piper after. Irina was carried out the front, but the others quietly went down to the basement toward a small exit on the side of the building.

"It's sort of weird," Piper commented as they left the Hermitage.

"That you're walking around a museum in St. Petersburg in your underwear soaking wet?" Peter asked.

"No. That people keep trying to kill me."

"Oh, that," Peter mused. "Sun rises in the east and sets in the west. Birds have wings, and elephants have a trunk. This is just one more of those every day for sure kind of things."

It turned out that the Americans had a safe house of sorts in a closed pizza place. They ushered Peter and Piper inside through a back alley. It was daytime, but the pizza place was dark. There were eight small tables, and the tiled floor was cracked and dusty. One of the military men gave Piper men's sweatpants and hoodie to wear, and she put the outfit on while everyone watched, which was disconcerting to say the least.

"Hard to find places without eyes and ears on us," one of the American operatives told Peter, gesturing to the pizza place. "That's why we're here. Your hotel is full of eyes and ears, for example. You won't have any privacy there. Even in the bathroom. So, remember that."

Ugh. Piper wanted to take a hot bath in private, but now that she knew cameras were everywhere in her hotel room, she was going to have do some sponge bath maneuvering. She had had enough of being mostly naked in front of strange men.

And sex was definitely out of the question while they were in the hotel. Peter seemed to be aware of that fact because he was looking at Piper with puppy dog eyes.

She crossed her arms in front of her. "Not even under the blankets," she told him.

Peter, Piper, and two of the American operatives sat at a small table. "That was a Russian assassin who almost killed you," one of them told Peter.

"We're used to it," Piper said. "Wherever we go, it's always *pow pow*."

"I figured she was Russian government issued," Peter said. "How did she know why we're here?"

It was a question, but Peter's tone was definitely an accusation. Piper hadn't thought of it before, but it was alarming that the Russians already knew who they were and why they were there. It meant that there was a leak on their side, and if it made the hair on the back of Piper's neck stand up, she could imagine what it was doing to Peter's spidey sense.

"Because our intelligence sucks balls, I guess," one of the Americans said, honestly. "But we did have eyes on you the whole time, so that should put you at ease. The point is that Russia's trying to hide whatever happened. We're talking about a nuclear incident, and we're in the dark, and they're obviously willing to kill to keep us in the dark. We can't get near the location of the nuclear isotope spike, and we can't hack into the Russian nuclear database. That department is locked up tight."

Peter and Piper exchanged a look, and Piper could read Peter's mind. He had to be thinking what she was thinking. They both knew someone who could hack into Russia's nuclear program.

The next day, Peter and Piper drove to a private airfield about a hundred miles outside of St. Petersburg. They parked by the airstrip, and a few minutes later, a plane landed. When it stopped, Peter drove up to meet it.

A door opened, and Adesh stepped out of the plane. He was carrying a small duffel bag and three computer bags. Peter opened his window, and Adesh waved at him, excited.

Peter helped him put his bags in the back of the car. "We have a place for you to set up," Peter told Adesh, once they were on their way.

"Already done," Adesh announced from the back seat. "I hacked into the Russian nuclear program while I was flying. You know, between lunch and my nap."

"You're amazing," Piper gushed, turning around to face him.

Peter looked in the rearview mirror and saw Adesh blush.

"It was easy to break in, much easier than hacking into 24 Hour Fitness. That was a bear to get into," Adesh said.

"Why did you hack into 24 Hour Fitness?" Peter asked.

"No reason," Adesh said, blushing again.

"What did you find out about the nuclear spike?" Piper asked.

"Nada. Whatever happened, it's been deleted or moved somewhere without a trace."

"Swell," Peter grumbled.

"So, nada?" Piper asked. "Like totally nada or nada with a side of something?"

"The only thing I picked up was a lot of searches of a museum with a pretty fancy jewelry exhibit happening in a few days in Italy," Adesh said.

Peter laughed. "How's that for a coincidence? More jewelry."

Peter didn't believe in coincidences. They had just found a murdered man in a gem museum, and now the Russian nuclear mystery was leading toward another gem museum in Italy.

"It's like we're magnets," Piper said. "We're like Elizabeth Taylor with marriages. Hey, I made a topical statement!"

"Good girl," Peter said. "It was topical for the over sixty-crowd, but it was still topical."

"So, what do we do now?" Adesh asked.

"That's simple," Peter said. "We find an anti-radiation suit."

CHAPTER 6

"You shouldn't be here," Peter chastised Piper.

"You shouldn't be here, either. If you're caught, you'll get shot for sure."

She had a point, but that didn't change the fact that this mission was designed for a superspy, not for a... well, whatever Piper was. Peter had used his contacts to find the location of the radiation spike, and he had done some pretty clever maneuvering to get close.

Peter and Piper stood under a tree in the middle of a huge fallow field, a few hundred meters away from an underground bunker, which was the site of the nuclear isotope spike. They couldn't get any closer without putting on their radiation suits, but Peter was having a helluva time trying to get his on. It was like a radiation suit for a rocket scientist or something. It was unnecessarily complicated. He couldn't figure out how to get it on right. He needed a manual or a PhD or a decent YouTube video.

"I'm not going to get caught or shot because I have superspy reflexes," Peter said, as he realized he had put the suit on backward.

Piper rolled her eyes.

"Did you roll your eyes at me?" Peter asked.

"Of course not. I don't roll my eyes. I'm a sophisticated, mature woman."

She rolled her eyes again.

"There! You did it again," Peter said and let the suit drop to the ground in frustration.

"Sorry, it was a natural reflex, brought on by witnessing your superspy reflexes trying to get dressed. You're putting that suit on all wrong."

"Everyone's a critic," he said. "I'm just distracted because you're not supposed to be here. It's dangerous."

Piper put her hands on her hips and rolled her eyes again. "I wasn't going to let you go alone, and I'm used to danger. Besides, I had to come. I'm the only one of us who knows how to put on a radiation suit."

Damn it, she was right. He had no idea how to put it on. He had thought it would be self-explanatory, but he was lost. He surrendered to her superior knowledge and let her help him. A couple of minutes later, they were both suited up. Piper carried a Geiger counter, and Peter carried an AK-47.

The radiation suit hood was claustrophobic, but once upon a time, Peter had spent two months imprisoned in a six-by-eight cage, so he could handle it.

"The Geiger counter is saying that radiation is above normal but not dangerous," Piper noted.

"Good. Above normal means the place will be deserted."

It was dark except for a full moon and a night sky full of stars. At three in the morning, Peter didn't expect a lot of pushback from Russian security, but he held tight to his AK-47, just in case.

The underground bunker had an entrance about a half-mile away, but Peter's source had told him about a secret way in through a sewage tunnel.

"It's not exactly safe to have an opening like this," Piper noted, as they started their trek through the tunnel.

"Maybe they have a comment card further on, and we can let them know. I'm sure they would appreciate your critiques. Are we going to discuss why you know how to put on a radiation suit?"

"I was hoping we would let that drop."

"You put it on like you've been doing it your whole life," Peter commented.

"I know. I wonder if that's part of the training to be a United Nations interpreter."

"I think we're going to have to let the interpreter theory go. I'm thinking your range of knowledge surpasses an interpreter's."

"I'm never going to find out who I am, am I?"

Peter's heart broke a little at the desperation in Piper's voice. He would do anything to make her happy and give her the answers she craved. It must have been horrible to lose one's identity. No matter who she used to be—or who she left behind and might want to reunite with—Peter would do everything in his power to bring her past back to her.

"You will," he assured her, as they continued down the tunnel. "I swear on my life that you will."

They walked for nearly an hour. No alarm sounded, and there was no sign of life. When they finally reached the end of the tunnel, they climbed a ladder to a hatch. Peter opened it after a struggle and climbed through.

After checking that the coast was clear, he helped Piper through, and they closed the hatch again. They were in the building, but Peter didn't know which floor or what they were even searching for.

They stood for a moment and listened. Nothing. It was a tomb.

A spooky, dark, cold tomb. It was like a scene out of a horror movie, and Peter paused a moment, half-expecting a zombie horde to attack. But there was no zombie horde or anything else.

They went down a dark hallway with cinder block walls and lined with doors every few feet. Peter checked them as they passed, but they were all locked. The only light was coming from the lights of their radiation suits. The Geiger counter had gone crazy as soon as they went through the hatch, and Piper kept checking it, while Peter watched for any sign as to what had transpired here.

It was the middle of the night, but Peter knew that a facility like this ran twenty-four hours a day under normal circumstances. Obviously, this wasn't normal circumstances.

"They bugged out pretty quick and pretty thoroughly," Peter said.

"It's like that movie you showed me."

"*I am Legend*. Yeah, that's what I was thinking too, except they didn't even leave behind a zombie."

They went up and down a few floors, but there wasn't a clue left behind. Piper's Geiger counter was lighting up like the Fourth of July, and Peter wondered if they had uncovered a new Chernobyl.

"We have to leave in seven minutes and get back

to the tunnel or risk radiation poisoning and death," Piper informed him, calmly.

"Okay. That gives me time to break into two rooms at random and then we can make a run for it."

But which door? It was impossible to know which would divulge anything like a meaningful clue.

"What was that?" Piper asked.

"What?"

"There it is, again. Don't you hear it?"

"No. Does radiation poisoning cause audio hallucinations?"

"There it is, again," Piper said. "A man is singing *Ochi Cherniye.*"

She pointed at a nearby room, and Peter tried the doorknob. It was unlocked, and he opened the door.

They stepped inside the room. It was piled high with filing cabinets and paper files strewn everywhere. In the center of the chaos was a small table, piled once again with paper files.

"Are you seeing what I'm seeing?" Piper asked Peter.

"No. I caught your audio hallucination, but it mutated into a visual hallucination."

"Oh, good. Me, too. I'm totally hallucinating."

It had to be a hallucination. There was no other reasonable explanation. Despite a facility-wide evacuation and off the charts radiation, there was still one man left in the facility, who was doing paperwork in a Kafkaesque office, practically drowning in dusty piles of paper.

Sitting at the small desk, an ancient-looking man with stooped shoulders and spindly arms was marking papers with an official red punch. He looked up without interest when Peter and Piper walked in.

Piper asked him something in Russian, and he blinked at her and smiled. She asked him another question, and he responded. He had few teeth, and a lot of hair growing out of his nose and his ears. He looked like he had grown onto his chair like a weed and he was stuck there indefinitely in shabby, baggy clothes.

"What did he say?" Peter asked her.

"I asked if he needed help, and then I asked him what he was doing here. He said I was beautiful. So, obviously, he's an intelligent man."

"Despite his choice to sit in a nuclear fallout area," Peter noted.

"I'll ask him what happened here," she said.

She kept the conversation quick in fluent Russian. The man seemed delighted to tell her everything since she was beautiful. He told her that there had been an accident, which he didn't know the details of because he wasn't a scientist. He was just a low-level bureaucrat who had worked and lived in the facility for many decades and had no fear of radiation. He was adamant that radiation wasn't dangerous and that folks made a big deal over nothing. When Piper insisted that he leave with them, he waved off her suggestion and gestured to the piles of papers that he needed to attend to. He refused to move from his home and place of work.

"He says that a scientist named Hans Schmidt was killed in the accident, but no one else. He says that Hans was a very old man anyway, so it wasn't much of a loss," Piper explained.

"Yikes. Cold," Peter commented. "If he insists on staying, that's all we can do here. Let's get going before we glow in the dark."

Piper said goodbye to the man, but he called her back and told her something.

"Now we can go," Piper said after the man finished talking, and Peter and Piper hightailed it out of there. They still had three minutes to make it back to the tunnel, but they didn't want to take any chances.

"What did the man tell you there at the end?" Peter asked Piper when they were safely back in the tunnel.

"He said that during the accident, some nuclear fuel went missing."

"What?" Peter asked, alarmed. He stopped in his

tracks and faced her to make sure he was hearing her correctly.

She nodded. "Missing nuclear fuel. He said it wasn't much, though."

"How much is not much when we're talking about nuclear fuel?" Peter asked. "Enough to power a Moonwatch? How much?"

"Enough for two bombs. Not the dirty kind. Real ones."

CHAPTER 7

Peter, Piper, and Adesh were back in the private plane on their way home. The revelation about the missing nuclear fuel had sent every American intelligence and defense agency into a tizzy.

It was all hands on deck to try and find it. That is, all except for Peter, Piper, and Adesh. They were persona non grata. Peter was even called an "amateur" and discounted by his two intelligence officers.

"They called me an amateur," Peter grumbled in the plane. He was lying on a couch with his head in Piper's lap. He had been wallowing in self-pity ever since they had been dismissed by American intelligence and escorted to the private airstrip.

"They didn't call you an amateur," Piper lied,

rubbing his head. "They just wanted to protect you."

"I don't want to be protected," he grumbled some more, sounding like a child.

"You don't need to be protected," Adesh said. He was seated in a recliner chair with an attached desk for his laptop. "You're a protector. Protectors don't need protecting."

Peter pointed at Adesh. "Exactly! Listen to Adesh. He's smart."

"I'm pretty smart, which proves that graduating high school is highly overrated," Adesh said.

"They wouldn't know about the missing nuclear fuel without me," Peter complained.

"And you wouldn't know without me," Piper reminded him. Men. They never grew up.

"Of course. Of course," Peter stammered, trying to backtrack. "You really saved the day."

"It's okay. It will all be all right," she told him absentmindedly while she rubbed his head.

Truthfully, she was caught in her own thoughts, completely obsessed with the mystery of the missing nuclear fuel. Why had it been stolen? When did the Russians discover the theft? Was the "accident" a ruse to steal the nuclear fuel? How did the "accident" happen and how did the scientist Hans Schmidt get killed? Where was the nuclear fuel now and who had it?

Piper squirmed in her seat. She tried to tamp down the antsy feeling, but her antsy feeling was way too strong. It was pulling her down into a deep rabbit hole filled with international villains, smuggling nuclear fuel in milk cartons, bent on the destruction of the world.

The rabbit hole was also full of images of mustachioed evildoers with guns and torture devices, and Piper pictured herself chasing after them, capturing them, and saving the day.

Yep, she was antsy.

She didn't know why she was like this. She had thought that she was only interested in mysteries and adventures and looking at death in the eye in order to save her own life and discover who she was and what had happened in her past.

But she had lied to herself. The truth was that Piper Landry got off on adventure. Peter may have been the retired superspy, but Piper had the obsession.

Her antsy feeling began to turn into a more determined feeling. She was upset that Peter had allowed the American authorities to handle the nuclear emergency on their own. Why hadn't Peter taken the reins? Why hadn't he gone behind their backs so that they could stay in Russia and run down the nuclear fuel instead of returning to San Francisco with their tails between their legs?

Was Peter losing his edge? Was he truly serious about retirement? Was his goal to be a suburban dad in khaki Dockers, never to save the world again? He had been in such a hurry to leave Russia and return home that Piper believed that he was ready to give up his old life and that his new life would be watching sports on television while he ate pulled pork sandwiches on the couch.

Piper didn't want that kind of new life, she admitted to herself.

"Holy shitballs, Piper. What's going on in your brain?" Peter asked, alarmed. She woke out of her thoughts. His head was in her lap, and he was looking up at her. His eyebrows were knitted together, and concern played over his face.

"Nothing," she said and gnawed on her lower lip.

"Something's going on in there. Something bad."

"You looked like you were going to send a complaint letter to George Lucas about Jar Jar Binks," Adesh agreed.

"Well," she started. How could she explain? She didn't want to upset Peter. "I might be a little peeved about something."

Peter sat up and faced her. "You said peeved. Nothing good can come out of that."

"Maybe not peeved. Maybe disappointed," she clarified.

"Oh, she means you, bro," Adesh told Peter. "You disappointed her."

Peter adjusted his suit. "Impossible. I've never disappointed a woman before," he said with a confident smirk. Then, the smirk disappeared as quickly as it appeared. "Have I?" he asked Piper, sounding like a child again.

"No. Yes. I mean, no. Yes," she said. "I just can't believe we gave up so fast and are returning home. There's stolen nuclear fuel out there."

Peter's smirk returned. "Oh, that. Well, the United States of America has some very fine intelligence services, not to mention a gargantuan military, so I'm sure they'll find the nuclear fuel, no problem."

Piper sat on her hands to squelch her antsy feeling and disappointment. "But they didn't even know about the stolen fuel until we told them. They would be in the dark without us."

"They have generals and drones and Navy SEALs with very little body fat," Peter said, counting on his fingers. "And they have phones, too."

"But they have a shitty computer system," Adesh added.

"But…" Piper started but clamped her mouth closed.

Peter took her hand and caressed her palm with

his thumb. "I get it. You like a little adventure in your life. You want to save the world again."

"Of course not," she lied.

"You want to risk your life. You want to see me save you once again with my lightning-fast reflexes."

"Certainly not that," she lied, again, pulling her hand away. She totally wanted to see his lightning-fast reflexes. She loved his reflexes. Peter had very talented reflexes.

"Hold on a second," Peter said and got up from the couch. He walked to the front of the plane and opened the cockpit door. He returned a minute later with the pilot. "Would you mind telling the woman I love where we're going?"

"Rome," the pilot answered.

"Rome? I thought we were going home," Piper said.

"Nope. We have a little detour. There's a museum with a certain jewelry exhibit opening in a couple of hours in Rome," Peter told her.

"The jewelry exhibit that the Russians searched for?" Adesh asked, excited.

"Bingo," Peter said, pointing at him.

His smirk had returned.

Piper felt a wave a relief, followed by a wave of love. She grabbed Peter and kissed him.

Rome never disappointed. Peter loved seeing the magical city through Piper's eyes. If she had ever visited Rome before, they didn't know, so everything was new for her.

They had checked into another no-name hotel, which offered off-the-charts luxury. They were shown to their suite with incredible views of the city and an expansive balcony.

They called for room service, and while Piper and Peter bathed, Adesh got to work on learning everything he could about the jewelry exhibit.

After Peter and Piper got dressed, they met Adesh on the balcony. Room service had arrived, and they ate antipasti while Adesh gave them the rundown.

"The museum is only a couple blocks away from here," Adesh told them. "It used to be some kind of palace for a prince. Then, Mussolini lived in it. After World War Two, the allies took it over for a year, and then it was empty for a few years before it was bought by Fiat, and twenty years ago, it was made into a jewelry museum."

"That's a building with a history," Piper noted and popped an olive into her mouth.

"Speaking of history, check this out," Adesh said, turning his laptop around so Peter and Piper could see the screen. There was a photo of an old man on it.

"Who's that?" Peter asked.

"That's Hans Schmidt, the scientist who died in the accident, and you'll never guess what." Adesh paused, as if he was waiting for them to guess the thing that they could never guess.

"He's a Jehovah's Witness," Peter guessed, playing along. "He's colorblind. He believes that the world is flat. He has six toes on his right foot."

Adesh scowled at Peter and closed his laptop. "Would you please get serious?"

Piper put her hand on Adesh's arm, and Adesh seemed to melt under her touch. "Peter's sorry," she said. "Tell us about Hans Schmidt."

"He's dead," Adesh said.

"We know that," Peter said. "He died in the accident."

Adesh shook his head. He was visibly excited, like he had a secret that was bursting to get out. "No, he was already dead. He died when the Russians invaded Berlin at the end of the war. Hans Schmidt was a Nazi."

Peter's skin tingled, and Piper leaned forward. "What do you mean a Nazi?" she asked.

"The kind that salutes the air," Adesh said and

illustrated with a Nazi salute. "The kind who wears a uniform. He was a nuclear scientist for Hitler, and he was killed when the Allies liberated Berlin."

Peter loved this story. He loved how the plot just thickened and how the adventure was just beginning. It made life interesting, like there were infinite possibilities waiting for him.

"But he didn't die," Peter said.

"But he didn't die," Adesh repeated.

"The Russians took him for their own program," Piper said, breathlessly. "They told everyone that he was dead."

"And they've had him all this time," Peter said. "That's a long-ass time. Poor bastard. He might have been relieved to die from the accident."

Peter tried to imagine the young Nazi scientist in Berlin, who had been captured by the Soviets. He had probably been imprisoned in the nuclear facility for decades. Poor damned Nazi. One minute he was happily working for Hitler, and the next thing he knew, Stalin had him by the short hairs.

"Anything else?" Piper asked Adesh. "What's the connection between the nuclear theft and the jewelry museum?"

Adesh shrugged. "No idea. I just know that the facility was Googling the museum like it was porn."

The three of them left the suite. The gold-carved elevator door opened, and they stepped inside. Peter let his hand glide down Piper's back and cupped her ass. She leaned back into his touch, and he didn't need any more invitation than that.

His arm circled her waist and drew her in for a happily-ever-after kind of kiss. Their tongues met as they devoured each other. Peter's body revved from zero to sixty, and it was all he could do not to take Piper right there in the luxurious elevator with Adesh taking up half of the small area.

"Oh, geez, bro," Adesh complained. "Can't you guys keep your lips off each other for five minutes?"

Peter tried to ignore Adesh's voice as he deepened the kiss even further. His body was on fire, and even though his brain knew objectively that the elevator was going to reach the bottom floor in a second and this would have to end, his pelvis had totally different ideas.

"It's like you guys have hormonal problems or something," Adesh continued.

Peter couldn't get enough of Piper. It was always this way with her. There was no end to his need for her.

"You should get that checked out. You might die from it," Adesh said. "Here we are. Thank God. It was starting to smell in the elevator, if you know what I mean."

Piper pulled back out of the kiss. She looked alarmed. "Smell? What're you talking about?"

Adesh stepped out of the elevator. "It's like living on the set of a porno," Adesh complained as he walked through the lobby.

Peter took Piper's hand, and they followed Adesh out of the hotel. "I like that," Peter said. "Set of a porno. It's good for my ego."

"Your ego never needed any help," Piper said. "You have a nice healthy ego. It's just like one of those turkeys fed with hormones until they're three times their normal size. That's your ego."

"I get the feeling that you're trying to insult me, but it's not landing," Peter said.

"I've noticed that it's very hard to insult you."

"I know, right? Nothing gets in," he said, tapping his chest. "I guess because I don't believe any criticism. And why should I?"

Piper elbowed him in the side. "It's a good thing I only believe twenty-five-percent of what you tell me. Otherwise, I would run screaming in the other direction."

"It wouldn't matter. I run faster than you. I would catch you again."

They walked the two blocks through Rome until they arrived at the museum. It was normal business hours, so they paid for tickets and entered. It was instantly evident that the museum used to be a palace. It was as ornate as the no-name hotel, but it was decked out in display after display of the most fantastic jewelry Peter had ever seen.

Adesh opened a map of the museum that they got when they entered. "What're we looking for?" he asked.

"I have no…" Peter began but stopped when he spotted four men walking out of the room they were in and into another one. "Let's go over there," Peter urged, following them.

"You've got that look in your eye," Piper said to him. "Like you're on to something. What're you on to?"

"Blonds. I'm chasing blonds."

"Excuse me?" Piper asked and ran a hand over her long red hair.

Peter sped up and found the group of blond men in the next room, talking among themselves. "They're very blond," Peter said under his breath. "Blond like a Nazi."

"Not all Nazis were blond," Piper whispered reasonably.

She had a point, but Peter thought it was too big of a coincidence that they had just been talking about a Nazi, and now he was faced with four men who looked like they had come out of Central Casting for a World

War Two flick. And here they were in a Roman jewelry museum. Was it a coincidence?

Peter didn't believe in coincidences.

"Look at that," Adesh said and jutted his chin in the blonds' direction.

Two of them had moved aside, revealing an old man talking to the two others. "Is that?" Peter began.

"Hans Schmidt, yes," Piper whispered.

"Damn it. The dead guy is alive again," Adesh said.

CHAPTER 8

"Let me see that map again, Adesh," Peter urged.

Adesh handed him the map, and Peter searched it to give him some idea of what the Nazis were up to. The map highlighted each room and its exhibits. After scanning the map, he saw a mention of a new jewelry exhibit. There it was. He found it. The new exhibit didn't sound like anything special. Gorgeous jewels in beautifully designed settings, but nothing quite as grand as the jewels in San Francisco. It was an odd avenue to follow for a nuclear fuel investigation, but after so many years as a spy, Peter knew never to discount a clue.

"You watch them. I'll be right back," Peter told Adesh.

The new exhibit was in another room, far away

from the Nazis. Peter found it in no time, a small room with beautiful jewelry and gorgeous stones.

"No provenance," Piper noted, reading the plaques next to the jewelry displays. She had, of course, followed Peter there. He hadn't noticed her following him at the time, but he wasn't surprised. Piper would never stay where there was no action, even if it was in a room full of Nazis. She was like a bloodhound on a scent wherever there was a mystery involved.

"Is that important?" Peter asked. "Provenance?"

"Provenance means where each work of art or in this case, jewelry, is from. These plaques only mention the designs and the details of the gems. There's nothing about where they came from. No work of art appears out of thin air. Art has history. A story. The story is what makes art important, especially jewels, I'm assuming."

She was right. The story was important and interesting. But for him, the lack of story was suspicious. Why would the museum omit it? Did it have something to hide? Were these necklaces, rings, and earrings so important that they had a secret that couldn't be divulged, or were they so unimportant that they didn't have a right to a history?

"The provenance is important. The story is important," Peter thought out loud, letting the idea roll off his tongue so that he could make head or tails out of it. But he came up empty. He didn't know why the exhibit was important. "We're missing a lot here, but I don't know what. It's like we're shooting in the dark. Let's go back to the Nazis."

"We still don't know if they're Nazis, Peter," Piper reminded him. "We just know that they're blond." She tapped her chin with her finger. "Although Hans Schmidt is with them, and he's a Nazi. Or was a Nazi. The Third Reich was a long time ago."

Peter took Piper's hand and started back to the other room. "Let's look at this situation a little closer. A Nazi is hanging around with a lot of young blond men with a disturbing lack of melanin in their skin. They're either Nazis, or Herr Schmidt is renting them for the night to remind him of old times. In any case, something is fishy. I'd bet my right nut that something's about to happen, and I refuse to miss it. There's too much on the line."

Of course, Peter didn't actually know what was on the line or if anything at all was about to happen. He would also have to admit to himself that he wouldn't really bet on his right nut, because of his two nuts, his right one was his favorite.

What did museum-quality jewelry with no provenance have to do with missing nuclear fuel? Nothing, as far as he knew. And was something really about to go down? Probably not, which meant that he was going to have to take matters in his own hands. He was going to have to get to the bottom of this international affair. He was going to have to take on five Nazis by himself.

Wow. He had always wanted to take on a bunch of Nazis.

Peter almost got goosebumps. It was like he was walking into *The Dirty Dozen* movie. And he was Charles Bronson. Or Lee Marvin. Yes, Lee Marvin. Lee was a kickass dude.

So, Peter was excited about beating up Nazis and forcing them to talk. It wouldn't matter which way it would happen, he was elated that he was going to get the chance to do it. He touched his jacket pocket to feel for his brass knuckles. Damn it. He had left them in San Francisco.

Just as Peter and Piper got back to Adesh, the lights went out. Light still filtered through the windows, but there was no electricity.

"Just like in San Francisco. They cut the electricity," Piper breathed next to Peter. She clutched onto him, as if she was worried that something was going to happen.

She was right. Something was going to happen.

Peter took his phone out of his pocket and shined

the light in the Nazis' direction. They were still in the room. He counted the four young ones and the old scientist. Just as he finished counting them, there was a loud crash coming from the other room.

An alarm sounded, and there were more loud noises from the other room, as if there was a fight going on. Piper pulled on Peter's arm.

"Aren't you going to go and see? Aren't you going to save the world?" she urged.

"Wait a minute," he said, calmly, never taking his eyes off the Nazis. "Wait a minute. This is just like David Copperfield in Vegas. This is Siegfried and Roy without the tigers. There's smoke and mirrors happening here. Sleight-of-hand. I can feel the manipulation going on, but I just can't figure out what's happening. All I know is we shouldn't trust our eyes or our ears."

Emergency lights came on, and the room was flooded with security guards. They told the visitors in Italian to exit the building. Peter was careful to keep the Nazis in his eye line and followed them to the exit. Outside, the police were arresting a man dressed in black.

"What a coincidence," Adesh said, watching the arrest. "He looks just like the dead guy in San Francisco. He's got the same outfit on, and he's real little like him. I could fit him in my pocket. I guess jewel thieves are small."

"You're right," Piper said, looking at the man. "He's a dead ringer for the man in San Francisco. What the hell's going on?"

Peter refused to look at the man. His eyes were fixed on the Nazis, standing together in a group a half a block down. He wouldn't even let himself blink.

Smoke and mirrors.

Sleight-of-hand.

Siegfried and Roy.

David Copperfield.

This was all a cheap Las Vegas act. Everyone was looking in one place, but the trick was happening somewhere else.

Don't watch the action, Peter thought. *No matter what happens, keep your eyes on the Nazis.*

Despite his will, a security guard got in Peter's face and started to yell at him, blocking his view of the Nazis. So much for good intentions. Peter knew a few languages, but his Italian was definitely rusty. Still, he understood the gist of what the security guard was yelling about. He wanted Peter to get in line. He wanted him to answer some questions.

Peter yelled back at the security guard and told him that he hadn't seen anything and to leave him alone. He stepped impatiently around the guard, but it was too late. Two of the Nazis were escorting Hans Schmidt into a black SUV.

"No," Peter said a little too loudly, as he watched the two Nazis climb in after the scientist.

The other two Nazis were still on the sidewalk. They locked eyes with Peter, and an unspoken threat passed between them. One of the Nazis slapped the car door twice and it began to drive away.

Sleight-of-hand. Don't look at the car. He stepped forward. He knew where to go. He knew where to look. He had found his target.

Peter rocked back on his heels and lunged forward, running full out toward the two Nazis. Unfortunately, they were running full out, too, away from him. Peter chased after them down the street and through an alleyway. They were fast and in shape. They didn't look military, but they were definitely trained.

Fucking Nazis.

Peter chased them for a mile, and just as he was about to reach them, they made a sharp right, opened a door of a cathedral, and ran inside.

Peter paused for a split second at the cathedral door, feeling slightly ashamed that he was about to breach the sacred building to do something decidedly unsacred. But the feeling passed quickly, and he opened the door and ran inside.

As cathedrals went, it was a small one. Dingy and

dusty. Completely abandoned as far as Peter could tell. Obviously, the Italian government hadn't gotten around to refurbishing it as it had with so many other monuments. The stained-glass was dark and dingy, and the stones were dirty. There were a few candles lit near the altar, but other than that, there was barely any light.

It didn't matter. There was enough light to see Peter's targets. The two Nazis were standing right in front of the altar at the end of the nave. They were facing Peter. Waiting for him.

Peter pulled his weapon out of his ankle holster, but they were also armed and shot at him. Peter dived into one of the pews while they let off another couple rounds. Peter crawled to the end of the pew and ran down the aisle on the side.

Peter knew that they were no match for him. He was an expert marksman and deadly in hand-to-hand combat. They were only two men. It would take a lot more than two men to best Peter.

"Give up now and save yourself," Peter called out to them. "You don't want to take me on. You're no match for me."

The Nazis let their arms drop by their sides. They were still holding their guns, but they were no longer aiming at Peter. Smart guys, Peter thought. They knew when they were outmatched.

Peter stood, walked up to them, and smiled. "Smart choice," he said. "Now let's talk about what's going on here. Tell me…" he started but was interrupted by the sound of footsteps on the cathedral's stone floor. Suddenly, the two Nazis were joined by six more.

Geez. Nothing was easy. Why couldn't things be easy? Peter thought.

Eight Nazis were a lot. Too much. Peter didn't even have that many bullets.

Or fists.

"What is this? An audition for *The Sound of Music*?" Peter asked. "Seriously folks, you guys need some sun, you know? Studies have proven that vitamin D is extremely important. But be careful of getting too much sun because then you'll burn and you'll get cancer and die. Although right at this moment, I'm thinking maybe I want you to die."

Peter raised his gun and began to press on the trigger, but one of the Nazis knocked the gun out of his hand.

And then they were all on him.

Eight men against one. Those weren't the best odds in the world. Peter had no help. No weapons. He had left his other gun and his knife back at the hotel for some reason.

Stupid, stupid, stupid superspy.

One of the Nazis punched Peter in the face, but he managed to punch him back, sending him to the ground. Another Nazi attacked him from behind, but Peter whipped around, took his attacker's back, and put him into a chokehold until he fell to the ground, unconscious.

With two of the men knocked out, Peter had enough time to escape them for a split second. He dodged another attack and ran to the other side of the altar. He searched for a weapon and found one.

"It was very thoughtful to have left this for me," he said out loud, finding a five-foot-long, brass cross. He wielded the cross like a monk in a really bad mood with some killer baseball training. One of the Nazis lunged for him, and Peter hit him over the head. *Whomp!* Then, he swung the cross again and hit another Nazi in the gut, which dropped him to the floor.

Peter wasn't big on religion, but maybe he would become religious now because the cross turned out to be one of the best weapons he had ever used. Nazis were dropping like flies.

One righteous man with a cross against eight Nazis. It would have made a great movie.

Peter barked laughter. "Look at me! You're no match for me and my big-ass cross. Get out while you can, you Nazi scum. Quit while you're ahead!"

Peter was about to say something else, something clever and threatening, just like Errol Flynn in *Robin Hood*, but he never got the chance to say it, and it turned out that he would never remember what he was about to say, because just at that moment one of the Nazis coldcocked him from behind.

Pistol whipped. That was the last thought that Peter had as consciousness left him, and he fell to the floor in inky darkness.

"Is he dead?" Peter heard. He could hear voices, but for some reason he couldn't see anything. Finally, he realized he couldn't see because his eyes were closed, and he opened them.

Ouch. Opening his eyes really hurt.

"Did I win? Did I beat the Nazis?" Peter croaked.

"I guess he's alive," Adesh said.

Piper was standing next to Adesh, looking down at Peter. She dropped to her knees and cradled Peter's head in her arms. "Are you all right? I thought we lost you. I thought they killed you."

Peter's head throbbed, but he had to admit to himself that he liked to hear the sound of panic about his demise in Piper's voice.

Peter struggled to stand. He saw black spots, but he took a deep breath in through his nose and out through his mouth and the spots went away.

"Of course, I'm fine. You should have seen me. I took on eight Nazis by myself. John Wayne never took on eight Nazis by himself. You know who's ever taken on eight Nazis? Nobody. Maybe Patton with one of his tanks. *Maybe*. But nobody else except for me."

Adesh looked from side to side. "That's awesome. Where are they? Did you bury them already?"

"They might've gotten away after they knocked me unconscious," Peter said, sheepishly. "But before that happened, you should've seen me. I ninja'd their asses.

Piper kissed Peter on the cheek. "Of course, you did. I'm very proud that you almost triumphed over eight Nazis."

Peter blinked. "So, you finally believe me about them being Nazis?"

"Yes, I do. I'm sorry for ever doubting you."

"Oh no," Peter said, slapping his forehead, finally understanding the situation. "I let them get away."

"But you were a ninja first," Adesh said, kindly.

"But I let them get away. They've gone without a trace. Our last lead has disappeared. We followed it to a dead end. Now there's no way of tracking them down. Not Schmidt. Not the other Nazis. Not the nuclear fuel.

What're we supposed to do? Go around asking if anyone has seen a bunch of Nazis in Rome? They'd put us away in a funny farm. Goddammit. Why didn't I bring my backup Glock? I wouldn't be in this position now. We would've had at least one Nazi in our custody, spilling the beans. But now we're in a total dead end."

"It's not that bad," Piper said.

"Are you kidding? We have no idea what the attempted jewelry heist was about except that the scientist was in on it."

"It wasn't an attempted jewelry heist. It was a successful jewelry heist," Piper said.

"But I thought they arrested a guy," Peter said.

"Right?" Adesh said. "This thing is all Twilight Zone-y, bro. They caught the guy, but the jewels were gone. *Poof!*"

"Definitely Twilight Zone-y," Peter said. "I have so many questions. Why was Schmidt at the museum? What does the jewelry exhibit have to do with the missing nuclear fuel? Where is the nuclear fuel? We don't know anything, Piper. That's the definition of a dead end. We don't know where the Nazis went, and we have no idea how to get to them."

"I know where they're going," Adesh said.

"That's true. Adesh does know where they're going," Piper said.

"Is that true?" Peter asked. Piper nodded yes. Peter hugged Adesh. "You beautiful, wonderful hacker. When we get home, I'm going to buy you all the Pop-Tarts your heart desires. What did you hack into and how did you find them?"

"I didn't hack into anything," Adesh said. He held up a leather mini-planner. "I found this in the bathroom. The cops let me go back into the museum after the arrest so I could pee. I figured the planner belonged to the Nazis."

He opened the planner to the first page. Sure enough, there was a swastika burned into the leather. "Yep," Peter said. "That's a pretty big Nazi clue."

"And the thing is, they filled in the planner," Piper said. "They're very organized. That's how we know where they went. They're going to Hawaii."

"I hear Hawaii is lovely this time of year," Peter said and smirked.

CHAPTER 9

Peter stepped out of the hotel bedroom, holding a few strings in his hand.

"What did they say?" Piper asked him.

Peter had been on the phone with the powers that be in Washington for the past twenty minutes. Piper could hear a little of his side of the conversation through the thick door, and none of it had sounded good. Peter was angry, which meant that the bosses didn't take the Hans Schmidt angle seriously.

"They told me that they're smarter than I am," Peter said with a strained voice. "I explained to them that the Nazi scientist is alive and that all of the Nazis are in Hawaii. I think I heard snickering on the line when I use the word *Nazi*, but I'm going to give them the benefit of the doubt and say they didn't laugh at me."

Piper sat on the couch. They were staying in a beautiful hotel room overlooking Waikiki Beach. Adesh was staying in his own room next door. They had arrived the night before, and Peter and Piper had made love with the windows open, enjoying the tropical breeze. Piper had felt totally relaxed in just the few hours that they had been there, but this conversation was changing all that.

"So that's it?" she asked. "They don't care anything about the Nazis? They don't care that the Nazi scientist is still alive and that he might know where the nuclear fuel is?"

Peter plopped down on the couch next to Piper and put his feet up on the ottoman. "No, they're going after the nuclear fuel all right. They seem to be very concerned about it, which is good. It means that they're not all morons. However, they're not coming to Hawaii and they're not sending anyone to Hawaii. In fact, they told me not to investigate at all in Hawaii."

Piper shook her head and tried to make sense out of what he was saying. "I don't get it. They're investigating, but they're not investigating?"

"They're investigating, but not in Hawaii. They told me that they have a lead on the missing nuclear fuel, and it leads them right to North Korea."

Piper leaned back and put her feet on the

ottoman next to Peter's. "North Korea? But the Nazis didn't go to North Korea. I'm not sure North Korea likes Nazis. North Korea is communist. The communists don't like fascists."

"Welcome to government work. It rarely makes sense," Peter told her and handed her the strings that he had been holding.

"What's this?" Piper asked.

"It's a string bikini."

Piper inspected the strings. She was surprised to discover that it was a bathing suit. It was mostly string, and there were three itsy-bitsy teeny-weeny patches of material, but it was still a bathing suit.

"What do you want me to do with this?" Piper asked.

"I want you to wear it. We're in Hawaii. Let's go out to the beach, and you can wear that, and I can look at you wearing it."

"I'm not going to wear this. It would be like having a walking Pap smear. I would be arrested. Worse, I would be a viral YouTube sensation."

"Please," Peter pleaded. "I've had a couple bad days. First, the Nazis got the best of me, and now the bosses won't believe me. North Korea… Like they can even get into North Korea. The only thing keeping me going is picturing you in that string bikini."

Piper handed the bathing suit back to him. "I'm glad that picturing it is keeping you going because that's all that you're going to be doing. Picturing it. I'm not wearing it. There isn't enough wax in the world for me to wear that thing."

"So, I'm not going to be able to see you in a bikini on a Hawaiian beach?" Peter asked, dejected.

"Oh, yes you are. I brought a bikini. It's hotter than hell. You'll have to keep your mouth closed so your tongue won't fall out."

It was hard for Peter to keep his mouth closed, but he tried his best because he didn't want his tongue to fall out. Piper was a sight to see on Waikiki Beach. She was the most stunning woman there, not that he was looking at any other women. Her body was womanly, with curves in all the right places. Her long red hair trailed down her back, making Peter jealous of it because it could touch her at all times.

They rented surfboards and took them out on the water. Piper believed that she knew how to surf. She didn't have a memory of surfing, but she had the feeling that she had surfed before.

"Maybe I was a professional surfer," she said,

carrying the board into the warm, turquoise-colored water. "I feel that I was. I can picture myself riding the waves. Hey, maybe I was on the cover of Surfer Magazine."

It was doubtful that she was ever on the cover of Surfer Magazine. She couldn't even get up on the board. She almost drowned twice, and when saltwater went up her nose, she panicked and Peter had to carry her back to shore. When she recovered, they decided to ditch the surfboards, and Peter body surfed with her for a while until Adesh showed up at the beach and urged them to come in for an early lunch.

After they ate a delicious dish of fish and rice, they drove to the west of the island to talk with one of Peter's sources. Jim DiMaggio was a retired spy, who used to work with Peter. He was slightly older than Peter, but he had retired years before his time because of an injury. They had kept in touch, and Peter knew that he owned a mixed martial arts studio on the island.

Even if Jim was retired, Peter was sure that he was still keeping tabs on the goings-on in the islands. If anyone had heard of Nazis being there, Jim would have.

The MMA gym was located in a strip mall about a block from the beach. There was a wall of windows that took up half of the gym and two open garage doors spanned the other half of the gym, revealing the gym to the outside.

They walked in through the front door and found Jim coaching a sparring match. Peter made eye contact, and Jim signaled to someone to take over his coaching session.

"Look at what the cat dragged in," Jim said, shaking Peter's hand. "I heard that you got fat and happy, but I didn't realize just how fat and happy." He winked at Piper.

Peter lifted his shirt to show off his washboard abs. "Happy but not fat. You have a minute to talk?"

Adesh and Piper stayed back while Peter spoke with Jim in his office.

"Well?" Jim asked.

"Nazis."

"Nazis," Jim repeated.

"Don't laugh. I'm looking for Nazis on the island."

"So that's who they are. Nazis. Makes sense," Jim said.

Peter leaned forward. "You've seen them? Where are they?"

Peter gave his former colleague the rundown about the Nazis and the missing nuclear fuel.

"I've heard of a strange group on a tiny island, which is accessible only by boat or helicopter. I heard there's some weird goings-on there. Dangerous stuff. Lots of blond guys."

Peter pointed at him. "Those are my guys. Nazis. How do I get there?"

Jim gave him the name and coordinates of the tiny island. "Be careful when you go. Watch your six at all times. The island is…weird."

"How weird?"

"You ever see the movie *The Island of Doctor Moreau*?"

"Yes. A horror movie. Doctor Moreau turned animals into people."

"This island is weirder than that."

They got to the helicopter pad, but all of the helicopters were grounded because of an incoming storm. Peter tried to bribe the helicopter pilot with a big chunk of Piper's money, but he wouldn't hear of it.

"I'm not risking my life and my license so you can visit that crazy place," the pilot said. "They say the storm might turn into a hurricane."

He directed them to a boat rental place, and they rented a boat with a GPS system. Peter plugged in the coordinates, and the three of them started on the three-hour boat trip.

"I don't know what they were talking about. It's smooth sailing," Peter said.

"Not a cloud in the sky," Piper agreed.

After about fifteen minutes, however, dark clouds rolled in, and the skies grew dark. The winds picked up, and so did the waves. The boat was rocked from side to side, and Piper was delighted to realize that she wasn't seasick at all.

"Hey, maybe I'm a sailor," Piper said. She liked the idea of being a sailor. Maybe she had sailed the seven seas. Maybe she had taken rich tourists around the Hawaiian islands in her boat. Maybe she was a Navy SEAL, just like Demi Moore. "I bet I dived, too. I can see myself diving in crystal clear water with sharks. I wonder if I like sharks. What do you think, Peter? Peter?"

"No, those pants don't make your butt look big," he replied. He was holding onto the wheel, trying to pilot the boat through the choppy waves.

"What? Why did you say that?" she asked turning her head to look at her butt. "I didn't say anything about my butt."

"Huh?" he asked. The boat crashed into a huge wave, and Piper fell onto a chair.

"You weren't listening to me. I was talking about being a sailor," Piper said.

"Great idea. If we survive this storm, you can be a sailor."

"I didn't say that, either. Why aren't you listening to me?"

Adesh moaned and hung his head over the side of the boat. Piper heard him retch, and then he flopped back on the chair next to her. He gripped her arm and looked at her, wild-eyed.

"We're going to die!" he screamed. His voice had risen a couple of octaves, and he sounded a little like Lady Gaga.

"We're not going to die," Piper assured him.

"We have a seventy-five percent chance of dying," Peter called from the helm of the boat.

"It's just a little rocky," Piper said.

"It feels like I'm trying to sail through a tsunami," Peter said.

Adesh's face turned purple, and he hung his head over the side again. Piper was so grateful that he didn't throw up on her.

She patted his back. "It's going to be okay. We're almost there."

"Unless we've been blown off course, and we're going to float through the entire South Pacific until we're desiccated corpses," Peter called back, raising his voice. It was still hard to hear him because the wind was building.

"I'm going to die. I'm going to waste away," Adesh moaned.

"You're going to be fine. We're almost there," Piper repeated.

"I'm no fool. I've thrown up twice. I only have hours to live. Maybe minutes," Adesh said.

"We'll get you some Gatorade when we get there," Piper said.

"*If* we get there," Peter called.

They got there.

Peter managed to dock the boat on a small pier. The island was tiny, and a small village hugged the coast. The clouds had rolled in and instead of looking like it was midday, it looked more like the middle of the night. The wind roared, blowing everything that wasn't tied down.

When they got off the boat, Adesh dropped to the ground and laid on his back. "I'm wasting away!" he moaned. "I'm never going to survive."

"Let's get you something to eat in the village," Piper suggested.

Adesh got up. "Sounds good," he said. "Where's Peter?"

They turned around to find Peter kissing the

dock. "I can't believe we made it," he said to the planks of wood. "I'm definitely going to start going to church."

When everyone was sure that they were still alive, they walked into the small village. There was a sign at the entrance.

"Aloha Wildlife Preserve," Piper read. "The island is a wildlife preserve. That's very nice. I like animals…I think."

"Does that mean they don't have food? Maybe all the food is protected," Adesh said, alarmed.

"I'm sure they have food," Piper said, but she wasn't so sure. As they walked toward the village, it was completely quiet except for the sound of things crashing into the small, squat wood buildings as the wind blew them.

A man walked by, and Peter tried to ask him a question, but he continued walking as if he didn't notice Peter.

"He didn't even blink," Adesh said. "He was like a zombie."

"There's no such thing as zombies," Piper assured him.

"Except for here," Peter said. "I think there's a definite possibility that there are zombies here."

"Zombie Island," Adesh breathed and looked around, as if he was afraid that a horde of zombies was going to jump out of the bushes and attack them.

"There's no such thing as…" Piper began but closed her mouth when another person walked by without taking any notice of them. No blinking.

Just like a zombie.

The village consisted of a few buildings. It looked like a Western town from the movies, except more tropical. They found a saloon halfway through the village and decided to go in for information and food for Adesh.

They began to cross the dirt road toward the saloon when three men on horseback trotted toward them. The men were wearing khaki uniforms and sidearms.

"Are those park rangers?" Adesh asked.

"They look military-trained to me," Peter said. "Guns for hire."

"Not more mercenaries," Adesh complained. "I hate mercenaries."

Adesh had had a bad experience with mercenaries. He blamed them for a cockroach incident that had left him with PTSD.

"I don't think they're mercenaries. I think they're a security detail," Peter said.

"For the Nazis," Piper guessed. "They're Nazi security."

A woman ran out of one of the buildings and into

the street. She screamed something unintelligible at the men on horseback, and they stopped in their tracks.

"Move aside, woman!" one of them yelled at her.

Piper saw Peter's body tense, as if he was preparing for a fight. But he didn't need to help the woman. Not only was she the first villager they had seen who was animated, but she could hold her own.

She screamed something else at the security guard, and when his horse took two steps forward, the woman balled up her fist, pulled back her lean arm, and let it fly. Her fist made contact with the horse's mouth, and it went down hard, trapping the rider's leg under it.

"She punched a horse," Peter said.

"She punched a horse," Adesh said.

"She punched a horse," Piper said.

Even though they all said it, they still couldn't believe it. The two other security guards hopped off their horses and helped their fallen colleague. The woman with the right hook walked calmly back into a nearby building.

"Zombie Island," Adesh said under his breath.

Peter, Piper, and Adesh crossed the street, walking past the guards, who got the horse up, freeing the man. When Peter, Piper, and Adesh got to the saloon, a man was standing in the doorway.

"She did it again?" he asked. "Lulu punched another one of their horses, huh? I told them not to come around here, but they don't listen. One minute it's a horse, and the next minute, she's going to stab them in the eye with a shrimp fork. You know what I mean?"

Piper didn't know what he meant. She thought it was very doubtful that the woman who punched a horse possessed a shrimp fork.

"I'm Frank. I own this establishment," the man said, introducing himself. "Come on in."

The saloon must have been more than a hundred years old, and Frank had probably been alive for most of that time. They sat at the bar, and Frank served them water.

"You look like you could do for some Pop-Tarts," he said to Adesh.

Adesh's mouth turned up in a wide smile. "How'd you know? That's exactly what I need. I have a glandular problem, and the boat ride over almost killed me."

Frank plopped a box of Pop-Tarts on the bar, and Adesh tore into it. There were a handful of other customers who were sitting at tables. They could have all been mistaken for zombies.

Peter leaned over and whispered in Piper's ear. "*The Walking Dead*. It's real. We're in it."

Piper shushed him. "Don't make any unnecessary movements or sounds. We don't want them to eat our brains," she whispered back.

"It's amazing you weren't killed," Frank told Adesh. "A fast-moving hurricane is on its way. It's due here any minute."

"A hurricane?" Adesh asked.

"A three-pointer," Frank said. "It's headed straight for us."

"We're looking for Nazis," Piper said, cutting to the point. She wanted to get off of Zombie Island as quickly as possible and back to their big, sturdy hotel before the hurricane hit.

"You mean the blond Europeans about a mile out?" Frank asked.

"Yes, that sounds about right. Where are they?" Peter asked.

"Strange group. Very secretive. The guards on horseback are theirs. We don't have cars on the island, you see," Frank said. "Those blond fellows like to keep to themselves. They never come into town. I guess they have their own supplies. That's fine with me. I heard they were weird, so we don't want them in town."

Peter choked slightly on his water, and Piper slapped his back hard. "Nope. You wouldn't want any weirdos here," Peter said.

Frank gave them directions to a tall, one-story cinder block building a mile east. Adesh was down to his last Pop-Tart, and they were about to get up to leave when a man walked in, dressed in a large potato sack and sandals.

"God!" he shouted.

"Not this again," Frank muttered.

"God! Hear me! God!"

"Did you hear that?" Peter whispered to Piper. "God."

"Convert to my religion or your soul will be damned!" he shouted.

One of the zombies sitting at a table seemed to rouse. "Shut up," he growled.

"You cannot silence me. God! Hear me! God!"

"This isn't going to end well," Peter muttered.

"Shut your face, or I'm going to filet your face!" the zombie barked. He had turned from a zombie to a psychopath in a split second. He wielded a butter knife like it was the perfect tool to use to filet a man's face.

"I'm not sure I want to see a man get his face fileted," Piper said to Peter.

"Really? I'm on the edge of my seat," he said.

"God! Save your souls and listen to me! God!" The man's potato sack fell off his shoulder, and he adjusted it.

"Shut the hell up!" the zombie yelled and waved his butter knife.

"Yeah, shut the hell up!" another zombie yelled.

"I am the only religion! I am the true religion! I am…"

The second zombie threw a glass at the true religion, and it landed square in his chest. "Shut the hell up! No one wants your bogus religion."

"I am love and light! I am the word of God!" he yelled back and pulled a gun out of his potato sack. Peter hopped off his stool and covered Piper just as the man in the potato sack shot the zombie in the gut.

"Wow, that's a tough religion," Adesh said and ate his last Pop-Tart.

It turned out that Frank was an MD, so he took care of the zombie's bullet wound without a problem.

"It's not the first time, and it won't be the last," he commented.

Peter didn't know if he meant it wasn't the first time the man had gotten shot or it wasn't the first time that the potato sack man had shot someone. Peter didn't wait around to find out. They needed to move on with their mission in a hurry. He, Piper, and Adesh walked quickly out of the village toward the Nazis' hideout.

Piper seemed to be in the most hurry. The

hurricane was approaching fast, and the rain had begun. If they were going to make it back to Honolulu, they would have to save the world on the double.

They found the building without a problem, despite the wind and rain. It was the only cinder block building, and the vegetation had been cleared around it. They stood a ways away, watching for movement, but the Nazis must have taken cover ahead of the hurricane.

"Well? Are we ready to take on the Nazis?" Peter asked.

"I'm ready," Piper said. "Are you?"

"I've got more weapons hidden under my shorts and aloha shirt than is even possible," Peter said. "I've defied physics. Neil Degrasse Tyson would be amazed."

They stepped forward toward the building.

CHAPTER 10

Peter wasted seven minutes trying to convince Piper to stay back, out of the line of fire, while the rain soaked them.

"There's no fire and no line," Piper pointed out and sprinted toward the building on her own. It was a stupid thing to do. Reckless. She half-expected to get shot while she ran. But it was the only way for her to get into the building. Peter was about to hog-tie her otherwise. He had been hyper-protective over her, lately, and it was annoying her. If Piper didn't know better, she would have thought that Peter was scared of Nazis.

It took a couple of seconds for Peter to catch up to her. "We're running right up to the front door, you know that, right?" he complained as they ran.

"We'll tell them we're the electric company."

"This is crazy. We're crazy. They're going to take away my superspy credentials for this."

"You're retired, remember?"

When they made it to the front door, Peter pulled Piper aside so that their backs were up against the wall next to the door. They watched as Adesh huffed and puffed toward them. When he got close enough, Peter ran out a few steps and pulled Adesh next to them.

"I ran through a hurricane," Adesh announced, euphoric. "I was just like an athlete. It's like I don't have a glandular problem anymore."

"Can we all shut up a little?" Peter asked, obviously frustrated. "How about we stop the coffee klatch until we've saved the world? We've literally announced to the Nazis that we're here. They're going to cream our asses."

"No, they won't," Adesh insisted. "'Cause we have you. You'll save us."

Peter pulled out a gun. "This is so stupid. We can't go through the front door. Give me a moment to figure out how we're going to take them by surprise."

"The front door's open. The wind blew it open," Adesh said.

They craned the heads in unison to better see the door. Sure enough, the door was wide open.

"Hear that?" Peter asked.

"I don't hear anything," Piper said.

"Exactly. Follow me, but be careful, for the love of God."

Piper followed Peter, and Adesh followed Piper. They stepped through the door. The building was wide open like a warehouse, except for a row of makeshift offices on the right side. In the back, Piper could see several rows of military cots.

Peter closed the front door, and they stood in place for a moment and listened. Nothing.

"They bugged out," Peter said. "They're long gone, and we have no idea where."

"Maybe they knew we were coming," Piper suggested.

"Maybe they knew about the hurricane, more likely," Peter said.

"Look at this," Adesh called. He had wandered off, and now he was pointing at something on the far wall.

Peter and Piper joined him and looked up at the wall. There was a giant swastika painted on it, and underneath was written *Fourth Reich* in bright red letters.

"What does it mean?" Adesh asked.

"It means they're batshit crazy," Peter said.

"And they have nuclear fuel," Piper added. The

Third Reich under Hitler caused World War Two. All that a Fourth Reich would need was one nuclear weapon. But there was no way this group could have anything to do with the German government. The Germans were now committed to peace, and they had completely renounced their dark past. These people had to be rogue and definitely batshit crazy.

There was a loud sound, and the front door slammed open again. Rain started to come into the building.

"I think the hurricane has reached us," Adesh said.

"We'll ride it out in here. It's a solid building," Peter said.

There was a loud creaking noise, and as if on cue, part of the roof fell in on the other side of the building. "I think that's what they call perfect timing," Piper said. "Or the evil eye."

"It wasn't my fault," Peter said.

The wind screamed, and another chunk of the roof caved in. Cinder blocks were no match for hurricane-force winds.

"You guys get out. I'm going to take a quick look around," Peter said, but Piper decided to take a look around too.

She rushed to one of the offices and opened a

door. It had been cleared out, just like the rest of the building. There was another loud noise, and the building started to crumble around her. Peter ran into the office, hooked her waist from behind, and threw her over his shoulder.

"Don't you hear that the building is falling apart?" he demanded and ran out through the front door while carrying Piper.

"Where are we going to go?" Adesh asked, outside. He had to yell to be heard over the storm. The winds were blowing trees and parts of structures through the air, and they had to duck to avoid being bludgeoned to death.

"We need to head back to the saloon. It's stayed intact all these years, so it'll survive this hurricane," Peter said.

"Let me down. I can walk," Piper complained. She was hanging upside down, with her hands on Peter's ass to stabilize herself. She lifted her head to see behind them.

"No," Peter said and walked toward the village.

"The blood's rushing to my brain. I could die like this," she insisted.

"I don't trust you. You'll run into the trees because you think you see a Nazi," Peter growled and walked against the wind toward the village.

"You're the one who sees Nazis everywhere. Not me."

But it was useless. Peter wouldn't put her down. Piper didn't think of herself as a damsel in distress, but Peter had gotten into the habit of saving her. She watched the hurricane batter the island behind them, as Peter and Adesh struggled to get back to town. Parts of buildings flew by, narrowly missing them.

"It's the *Wizard of Oz* back here!" Piper shouted.

"It's the *Wizard of Oz* up here, too!" Adesh yelled and gasped for air, as he strained to keep walking.

"The good news is that it can't get any worse!" Piper shouted.

Behind them, Piper watched as the brush seemed to collapse in on itself. Whereas before debris flew into the air, this time it was like the earth had opened up and was swallowing all of the island's vegetation.

"Something bad's happening!" Piper yelled.

"Your powers of observation are one of the reasons I love you!" Peter yelled back.

"Something really bad!"

"You said it couldn't get any worse!" Peter yelled.

Piper wiped her eyes so she could see better. Whatever was swallowing up the island was getting closer. Through the rain and the wind, she could swear that she could see smoke. She wiped at her eyes again.

"That's not smoke! That's...Oh my God!" Piper yelled.

"Calm down. We're almost there!" Peter yelled.

"Animals!" Piper shouted. "Stampede!"

"What?" Peter yelled.

"Stampede! Big animals! Really, really big!"

Peter stopped running for a second and turned around to see what Piper was yelling about. "No way," he said. "No way in hell."

"What are they?" Adesh asked.

"Buffalo! Buffalo! Run for your lives!" It was the woman who had punched the horse. She was running for her life, just ahead of the buffalo. "The buffalo are stampeding from the preserve!" she yelled as she passed them.

Peter let Piper down, and they all ran for their lives, following the woman with the mean right hook.

The sound of hundreds of hooves hitting the ground nearly drowned out the sound of the hurricane. The three continued to run, just ahead of the buffalo.

"My glandular problem is back!" Adesh yelled in a panic. "It's back in a bad way!" But he managed to keep up with them. It was amazing what fear of death could make a person accomplish.

The whole time they ran, they followed the woman who had punched the horse. Just as they were about to reach the village, she pointed to the right and made a quick turn. They followed her.

The detour didn't work. The buffalo followed them. They were headed for the dock, running parallel to the village. The hurricane continued to batter the island, and the winds threw debris, making them duck and weave while they ran. But the immediate threat wasn't Mother Nature. The immediate threat was hundreds of terrified buffalo trying to run from mother nature.

"The water! The water!" the woman yelled.

They were close to the water, but it was a toss-up whether they could outrun the buffalo in time. Piper looked over at Adesh. She was worried that he couldn't keep up, but he was still running.

Finally, they made it to the water. "Under the dock!" the woman yelled.

"We're going into the ocean during a hurricane?" Peter asked.

But they had no choice. There was no other place to go. They all jumped into the water and swam under the dock. They held onto the pilings while the water rushed over them in heavy waves. In a matter of seconds, the buffalo found the water, too.

In a blind panic, they stampeded into the water. It was a horrible sight. The buffalo struggled to swim as their fellow buffalo fell on top of them. The animals cried out as they realized that they were in mortal danger.

"They're all going to drown," Piper cried, horrified.

"Stay here," Peter said. He climbed up the piling and flipped his body over the dock.

"Your boyfriend's abandoning you," the woman told Piper.

She was right. He totally was. "No, he's not," Piper said. "He wouldn't do that."

"He would never do that," Adesh said, coming to his friend's defense. "He's…what's that sound?"

"Wake up, big man. It's the sound of a hurricane and two hundred buffalo dying," the woman sneered.

"I hear it too," Piper said. It wasn't the sound of the hurricane or the buffalo. It was a motor.

The three peeked out from under the dock. Peter had found a Jet Ski and was motoring away from them.

"Men are all the same, baby," the woman said to Piper sympathetically as they watched Peter Jet Ski away. "A man once threw me out of a moving car."

"That's terrible," Adesh said.

"It worked out. I ducked and rolled. Then, the next day I broke into his house and cut his dick off," she said.

"That's…uh…" Adesh said and drifted off, as if he was lost for words.

Piper was barely paying attention to the conversation. She was focused on Peter, Jet Skiing away from her. She couldn't believe her eyes. Could it be that her knight in shining armor had turned tail and left her in the water during a hurricane?

As she watched, Peter turned the Jet Ski around and drove toward the dock in a zigzag direction.

"Is he drunk?" the woman asked.

"No, he's heroic," Piper said, understanding what Peter was doing. "He's saving the buffalo. He's risking his life in a hurricane in order to herd the buffalo back to shore."

As Peter worked to corral the buffalo, the hurricane began to die down. The wind slowed to a tropical breeze, and the clouds moved, revealing the blue sky. Peter's job to save the buffalo took a long time, but it worked. When he was done, all of the buffalo but two had made it safely back to shore. Now calm, the buffalo returned inland, as if nothing had ever happened.

When it was safe, Piper, Adesh, and the woman with the mean right hook swam out from under the dock and swam to the beach where they all laid down on the sand and caught their breath. Peter returned the Jet Ski and joined them.

"Good job, John Wayne," the woman told Peter. "I thought you were a dog, but you're a lion."

"Thank you, ma'am," he said.

"Call me Daryl," she said.

"I hate exercise," Adesh whined. "I feel like I'm going to die. Exercise does that. It's very dangerous. If you move the blood through your body too fast, it moves the cancer cells around and kills you."

"I'm not sure it works that way, bro," Peter told him.

"Nah, he's right," Daryl said. "I've heard the same thing."

"What a total waste of time. We got nothing," Peter complained.

"Why are you folks here, anyway?" the woman asked. "This island isn't in any tourist brochure."

"We were chasing Nazis," Piper said.

Peter slapped his forehead. "Seriously, Piper, we need to have a discussion about secrecy."

"Is that who those people were? The blond ones?" Daryl asked. "They kept to themselves, and they were slap-happy about their security patrols. But that didn't stop me. I have a houseful of their stuff."

Peter and Piper sat up straight. "What did you say?" Piper asked. "You have a houseful of their stuff?"

When they had recovered, they followed Daryl to her house. It turned out that she lived in a shack in the jungle, and like a miracle, it was still standing after the hurricane.

"Those Nazis bugged out a few hours before you folks showed up," she told them as she put a kettle on the stove to boil for tea. "I've been stealing from them ever since they showed up. I was over there today to see if they left anything interesting behind, but they cleared it out. Then, I was collecting coconuts when the shit hit the fan and the buffalo went mad."

"What kind of stuff did you steal from them?" Adesh asked. Daryl put a few mugs on the table and filled a teapot with tea and hot water.

"Pretty much everything. This teapot. Those mugs. The chairs you're sitting on," she said.

Peter and Piper locked eyes, and Peter smirked.

"How about a mini leather planner? Did you steal one of those?" Piper asked.

"Oh, yes. It's a beauty. I was going to give it to my niece for her birthday, but it's filled out, already. I got it here somewhere."

CHAPTER 11

"You know what? I'm never going to judge a person based on my first impression again," Adesh said. He, Peter, and Piper sat at a table in an outdoor café in Buenos Aires.

The weather was lovely, despite the bad pollution. There was a nice breeze that blew through Piper's hair, which felt delicious against her bare shoulders. They had arrived the night before, and she had already bought three outfits, including the red strapless dress she was wearing now.

Buenos Aires was an intoxicating city. Gritty. Sexy. Sensual. Even though they had come there to find the Nazis and the nuclear fuel in order to save the world, Piper couldn't help feeling that she was on a romantic vacation with Peter.

As Adesh spoke, she could feel Peter's hungry gaze on her. When she turned her head to face him, her suspicions were confirmed. He had been studying her, and his eyes were dark and full of desire.

He took her hand and placed it on his lap. He held it there, caressing her palm, which made her half-mad with arousal.

"I've found that my first impressions are always dead-on," Peter said to Adesh. "For instance, when I first saw Piper, I thought to myself: here's a woman with a bangin' bod."

"I was naked when you met me," Piper said.

Peter smirked. "But I appreciated your nakedness."

"I was thinking about Daryl," Adesh said. "When I first saw her, she punched a horse, and I thought: Now, there's a psychopath. But it turned out that she was a nice lady. She saved our lives and gave us the planner so that we could find the Nazis in Buenos Aires."

"You're right. Daryl's a nice woman," Peter agreed. "It was thoughtful of her to have systematically stolen most of the Nazi headquarters' supplies."

"I wonder how she got the table and chairs out of there without being seen," Piper said. "It had to be conspicuous. It was a big round table. I would have thought those mounted security guards would have spotted her carrying it on her head for a mile through town."

"Maybe they did spot her, but she punched their horses," Adesh said.

"And all of that copper pipe she pulled out of there," Piper continued. "That takes a certain amount of skill. And noise. I may be wrong, but I think we're dealing with less than smart Nazis."

"Hence their political choices," Peter said.

"But boy, are they organized. Each Nazi gets a leather mini-planner. That's nice," Piper said.

"It would have been nice to get one computer," Adesh grumbled. "This mission has been way too analog. I'm getting Dark Web withdrawals. I don't know if Daryl didn't want to steal a computer, or if Nazis don't like computers."

Peter stuck a finger in the air. "I've heard that there were very few computers in World War Two."

"That just doesn't make sense," Adesh said. "How did they expect to conquer the world without a computer?"

"I heard that Napoleon had the same problem," Peter noted.

Peter was joking, but a computer would have definitely helped them find the Nazis. The planner had gotten them to Argentina, but they didn't have an address.

"We don't know where the Nazis are. We don't have a lead on the nuclear fuel," Piper said.

The waiter came to their table and took their orders. "Excuse me," Peter asked him. "Do you know where we can find Nazis?"

"This is Argentina. Throw a ball, and you'll hit one. They came here after the war," the waiter said.

They ate grilled meats, yellow rice, and vegetables. After, Adesh decided to return to his digital roots at the hotel and see if he could dig up Nazi chatter on the web in order to give them more of an idea of how to catch them.

"Do you hear that?" Peter asked Piper when Adesh had left.

"What?"

"We're alone. Just you and me and Buenos Aires. That's the sound of a romantic date."

Peter was smiling at Piper, and it was contagious, like a happiness virus. She was helpless not to smile back at him. "I like romantic dates," she said. "What do you have in mind? How romantic? What're we talking about? Flowers?"

Peter took the rose centerpiece off the table and handed it to her.

"Music?" she asked.

A man with a guitar came out of the restaurant and took a seat in front of them.

"You didn't plan that," Piper said.

"No, I didn't, but let's pretend I did so it's even more romantic."

The guitarist began to play tango music, and a couple of dancers came out in full tango dress and began to dance.

"How about that? Did you plan that?" Piper asked Peter.

Peter pulled Piper onto his lap and kissed her neck. "Since I met you that night in the middle of the forest when you were stark naked and running for your life, nothing has been planned. Not one second of one minute. And it's been glorious. I'm the luckiest man on earth. Also, my one-eyed Uncle Joe is pretty happy, too."

"Your one-eyed Uncle Joe? Is that what we're calling it, now? Makes sense. He's sort of wrinkly, and I can picture him sitting on a recliner all day watching sports on TV."

Peter sucked air through his teeth, like he was in pain. "Recliner? Like relaxed and slouched? That was too much, Piper. You've insulted my manhood."

"What can I tell you? You were the one to call your manhood your one-eyed Uncle Joe. It all fell into place after that."

"Okay. Okay. You're right. From now on, we will call my manhood Rock Hardplace. Deal?"

Peter didn't give Piper a chance to respond. His Rock Hardplace was poking her, and his lips touched hers with the softest touch, making her mad for more. His strong arms wrapped around her, letting her know that he would never let her fall. But his lips told her that he would love her always like she was the greatest thing that had ever happened to him and that he knew it.

So, she loved his lips and made love to his lips. They were capable of giving pleasure, but in times like these, they conveyed a message which made Piper's head spin and her heart full, like someone who knows that no matter what, there's someone in the world who loves them and would do anything for them.

It was a heady message for a pair of lips.

Piper kissed him back, lightly grazing his lips so that she could barely feel the touch, but enough to feel the electric current between them. The electricity went through her, making her feel alive and making her core throb with need. They kissed like that for a while. Piper was dimly aware of the music playing, of the sound of the dancers' shoes on the cobblestones, of the crowd in the café. But it didn't slow the kiss.

It was only after the music stopped for a moment

that Peter pulled back. "It's like I won the lottery," Peter told Piper. "Not a scratcher. The real one where no one wins for months, and it grows really big."

"Like Rock Hardplace?" she asked and laughed.

"This thing between us," Peter started. "It's special. Not special. I mean, yes special, but special is a dumb word…"

"What're you saying?"

"Only that…" he started, but the dancers interrupted him. They said something in Spanish, and put their hands out to them. They wanted Peter and Piper to tango.

"I've always wanted to tango," Piper told Peter.

"You have? You remembered something?" Peter asked.

"No, but I just *know*."

"Like the surfing? Like that?" he teased, but he lifted her off his lap, and he stood. The guitarist began to play, and Peter pulled Piper into his arms.

"Let me lead," he whispered in her ear.

"Don't I always?"

"No. Never. You've never let me lead."

He was right. She had never let him lead. She always tried to lead, and then he had to save her. "Maybe I'll let you lead."

"If I don't lead doing the tango, we'll look pretty

funny," Peter warned.

"I promise I'll try to let you lead."

He spun her around into a tango that took her breath away. She didn't know the moves, but she allowed herself to take his physical cues, and they fell into a sensual dance. They had made love many times, but during the tango, Piper really felt like they were one. Joined. One soul and one heart.

"We're going to have lots of sex now, right?" Piper asked, as she and Peter walked back to their hotel after their tango. "Like a sex binge? Like a Netflix binge but with sex?"

"Oh, yes. Netflix has nothing on us, baby doll."

"We should do a tango position. Is there a tango position?"

"Yes," Peter said. "It's like the reverse cowgirl with a missionary twist."

"That sounds good. I like the sound of that."

"Although," Peter began. "There's a good possibility that Adesh has set up a hacking station in the living room of our suite, so our sex binge could get awkward."

"That would put a wrench in the works. But

Adesh is probably sleeping. We've done a lot of flying lately, and he's got jet lag."

Peter wanted to believe that, but he knew that Adesh would never sleep if he was on the trail of Nazi chatter on the web. He had enough Pop-Tarts packed in his suitcase to last all night.

"Maybe we should get a new suite," Peter suggested.

"Let's take our chances. If he's up, we'll figure it out."

When they got to the door of their hotel suite, Peter said a little prayer that Adesh was asleep so he could have a sex binge with Piper. Then, he put the key card in the door and opened it.

"Adesh," Peter whispered, checking to see if he was asleep.

"Not Adesh," he heard, and a man put a gun to Peter's temple.

Peter was about to disarm the man when he noticed that another man had a gun to Adesh's head, and yet another had pulled Piper into the room and was holding her.

They weren't blond, and they were definitely military. Peter wasn't fast enough to save both Piper and Adesh.

CHAPTER 12

It was during times like these that Peter wished he had never retired. If he was still an active spy, he wouldn't be traveling with a lover and a friend. He wouldn't have to think twice. He wouldn't have to put his hands up and relinquish his weapon.

If he were an active spy, he wouldn't be in love, and his heart wouldn't be breaking that a woman had a gun to her head. Her beautiful head with her breathtaking eyes looking at him, as if she expected him to save her and was honestly shocked that he was surrendering.

Another man entered the living room from one of the suite's bedrooms. He was older than the other three men, probably the man in charge, and he was eating a

Toblerone bar.

"I found your mini-fridge," he told Peter. "I have a sweet tooth. My wife's on me to lower my triglycerides, but I have to do something for the stress. I don't drink, so it's chocolate."

"What do you want?" Peter asked. He didn't really care what they wanted, but he needed to waste some time while he came up with a plan.

The man with the Toblerone sat on a chair by Adesh. "The question is, what do you want? That's why we're here."

Peter squinted at him. "Hold on. I know that accent."

"You should. And you should know the face. You came to my country for some training ten years ago when you were a young pup."

"Moshe?" Peter asked. "Jesus Christ."

"Jesus Christ? No, wrong religion my friend. Holy Moses is more like it."

He was Colonel Moshe Shaitrit of the Israeli Defense Forces. The last time Peter had seen him, he was in charge of an elite commando unit, and he had trained Peter how to kill a man with a Q-tip. It was a skill that had come in handy a couple of times in his career.

"Colonel. It's been a while. Nice to see you, again. We're all friends here. Israelis and Americans.

Americans and Israelis," Peter said. "Why don't you put your weapons down."

"Just as soon as you tell us what you're doing here. I heard that you're looking for Nazis. I just want to make sure you're on the right side."

"Is that what you're doing these days? Are you Nazi hunting? I can assure you that we're doing exactly the same thing."

The Israelis had always had a group on the hunt for Nazis, ever since the end of the Holocaust. They had scoured the world to bring to justice those who had committed heinous crimes against the Jews. Their most daring success was finding Adolph Eichmann in Argentina. They had abducted him and brought him to Israel to stand trial.

These days, there were few Nazis still alive, and Peter had believed that Israel's Nazi hunting days were far behind it. But if Colonel Shaitrit was involved, it must have still been a priority for the Israeli government.

Despite the gun to Peter's head, it was good news for him.

"Who are you after?" Moshe asked.

"Hans Schmidt."

Moshe signaled to his men, and they holstered their weapons. Peter took Piper's hand and helped her sit on the couch.

"Sorry about the guns, my friend," Moshe said. "We just needed to make sure we weren't at cross purposes."

"Are we?" Peter asked.

"No. We're not looking for Hans Schmidt," he said, taking another bite of the Toblerone. "Hans Schmidt is dead, my friend."

"No, he's not," Adesh said. "He was taken by the Soviets at the end of World War Two."

"We know that," Moshe said. "But he died recently."

Peter smiled. He loved knowing more than the Mossad. "We saw him in Italy. We think he's here with a band of blond Nazis. We'd love your help."

One of Moshe's men laughed.

"He's telling the truth," Piper said. "There's a bunch of young Nazis with him."

"What the hell are you talking about?" Moshe demanded.

Peter told the Israelis all about it. All except for the missing nuclear fuel. That information was the property of the Americans, and he wasn't willing to cross that line. But it was enough for the Israelis.

They didn't think a group of young Nazis was anything to worry about, and any ideas about a Fourth Reich were ridiculous, according to the Israelis. But

Moshe was willing to help a former colleague. So, he gave them the coordinates of a Nazi meeting happening the next day.

"You won't find what you're looking for at tomorrow's meeting. It's purely for lowlife losers who can't get a date," Moshe warned Peter. "But who am I to prevent someone from taking up Nazi hunting. In fact, I wish the whole world would do it."

He and his men began to leave the suite, but Peter stopped Moshe with a hand on his arm. "You didn't say what you're doing here. What kind of Nazi hunting are you doing?"

"Bigger than a dead scientist, my friend," Moshe said and winked.

The Nazi meeting was taking place in an elementary school at night. The Israelis gave Peter the code word to get in.

"Tinkerbell is a weird code word," Piper noted, as she approached the school's cafeteria with Peter and Adesh.

"I've had weirder," Peter said. "White supremacists seem to have the most warped views of themselves. There was a group in Idaho who had imprisoned five eleven-year-old girls to be their frontier wives that I had to infiltrate and take down. Their code word was Sweet Pea."

"The real world is nothing like an Arnold Schwarzenegger movie," Adesh said, wisely. "He would never say sweet pea or Tinkerbell. He would say a cool line, filled with testosterone and coolness."

"I wonder if I've ever seen an Arnold Schwarzenegger movie," Piper said. Adesh and Peter stopped walking and stared at her like she had sprouted a second head.

"We have to change that," Peter said.

"No *True Lies*? No *Predator*?" Adesh asked, aghast.

"We have to change that right now. Let's go back to the hotel," Peter said seriously. "Forget the Nazis and nuclear destruction. You need to see *Conan the Barbarian* immediately. That movie inspired me in a lot of different ways."

Piper pointed at the door to the cafeteria. "Our popcorn-eating movie watching has to wait until we break up the Fourth Reich and reclaim the nuclear fuel before something blows up."

"Popcorn sounds good right now. I like a little popcorn after dinner," Adesh said.

"The kind with butter-flavored popcorn salt,"

Peter agreed. "Not the organic natural kind from Whole Foods. That stuff is crap."

Adesh nodded. "The preservatives add flavor. Butter needs preservatives to taste like butter. Otherwise, it doesn't taste real."

Peter high-fived Adesh. "What he said."

"Can we get back to the Nazis?" Piper pleaded.

"I bet Nazis don't eat popcorn," Adesh said. "I bet they don't even eat when they watch Schwarzenegger movies."

"That's it," Peter said. "If that's true, these madmen must be stopped!"

Piper rolled her eyes. "Maybe I should go over to the Nazis' side. I bet they don't waste time talking about popcorn and movies. I bet they're studiously keeping to the topics of mass genocide and world domination, like sane, mature people."

Peter arched an eyebrow. "Was that a joke?"

"Yes, of course. If we can't do Nazi humor, we might as well give up now," she said. She knocked on the door, and a young man with a shaved head opened. He scowled at the three of them, and they smiled back at him.

"Tinkerbell," Piper said.

"You're a woman," the skinhead complained.

"Tinkerbell," Peter repeated, and Piper could

have sworn he flexed every muscle in his body. She was with him all the time, so she had gotten used to his size, but for everyone else, he was an imposing six-foot-six behemoth of a man. A walking threat. The skinhead flinched and stepped back.

He opened the door, and the three of them walked in. The cafeteria's tables and small chairs had been pushed against the far wall and had been replaced with adult-sized chairs, which had been placed in rows facing the kitchen.

Banners of swastikas and Hitler covered over pictures of children eating balanced meals and the four food groups on the walls. There were at least fifty people in attendance. Piper scanned the room for the blonds and found one walking through a door in the far corner.

"People are looking at me," Adesh whispered.

"Well, you cut a fine figure in your cargo shorts," Peter said.

"I got them from JCPenney. You don't hear much about that store anymore, but it's got killer deals."

"They're looking at you because of your skin color," Piper pointed out.

"That's rude," Adesh said. "That's racist."

"Shocking for Nazis. We should make them take a cultural sensitivity class," Peter said.

"I saw a blond go through that door," Piper said,

gesturing with her head.

"Stay here. I'm going to mix and mingle," Peter said.

Normally, Piper would have gone with him, but she wanted to stay with Adesh, in case the Nazis gave him trouble. Sure enough, as soon as Peter left their little group, two of the Nazis came over and got in Adesh's face.

"How did this towel-head get in here?" one of them demanded in a drunken sneer.

"Towel-head? That's socially insensitive," Adesh said.

"Huh?" one of the Nazis said.

A man in an SS uniform stood at the front of the room and called the meeting to order, but the two Nazis didn't leave Adesh.

"The meeting's starting," Piper said, which only served to draw their attention to her. She was the only woman in the room, and she wondered if these new Nazis had added women to their hate list.

"How did a towel-head get in here?" the other Nazi demanded.

It was getting tense, and if the situation wasn't diffused soon, their cover would be blown. Piper wracked her mind for a way to diffuse an awkward social situation with Nazis, but she came up blank.

"I'm not a towel-head," Adesh repeated, doing his best impression of a Texas accent. "And I'm not Indian, so don't even think that I am. Not at all Indian. *Blech*. I hate Indians," he said and spit on the floor for emphasis. "So, don't even think I'm Indian. I have a glandular problem, and it's made my skin darker. But I'm planning on getting a laser peel, so this will all be in the past soon. Yay, white people! Yay, white people!"

Piper took Adesh's hand and pulled him away. The meeting started. The Nazis sat in the chairs and listened to the speaker, who was speaking in Spanish. Piper and Adesh walked along the wall until they got to the doorway where Peter had followed the blond.

"That was upsetting," Adesh said. "Very politically incorrect. I bet that somehow my mother heard what I said about India, and she's cursing me right this second. We probably shouldn't do this. It could be dangerous to go in through that door," Adesh said.

"You could stay with these Nazis so you could tell them more about how you're not Indian," Piper suggested.

Adesh blinked. "Maybe you're right. Let's find Peter."

They found Peter in what looked like the kindergarten room. He was up against a wall, getting beaten up by a group of blond Nazis.

"I'm fine," Peter called to them and was punched in the nose.

Piper hoped they didn't ruin his nose. Peter had a beautiful straight nose. She loved his nose.

"Totally fine," he called again, and they punched him in the stomach. He doubled over and spit blood.

"Leave my friend alone!" Adesh yelled and ran into the fray.

He tripped on the activity rug on the floor, running into the Nazis like a bulldozer. He took three Nazis down as he fell on top of them. Peter took the moment to jump away from the wall and start punching wildly at two other Nazis.

"You seem to have this under control," Piper said and looked around for Hans Schmidt. She was certain the scientist was the key to all of this, and if they found him, they could get him to tell them where the nuclear fuel was.

Peter continued his slugfest while Piper spotted a door by the hamster cage. She assumed the door led to a supply closet.

"Totally fine. Don't need any help," Peter called after getting kicked in the head.

Piper opened the door. She had been right. It was the supply closet. Inside, Hans Schmidt was hiding. No, not hiding. His face was etched in fear, and his wrists were bound with duct tape.

Hans Schmidt wasn't in on the Nazi conspiracy. Hans Schmidt was being held captive.

"Sonofabitch. No, I'm totally fine," Peter called.

She turned around to see him whack a Nazi's head with a tiny chair. Adesh rolled off the three Nazis, and they began to rouse. Peter threw a small coat rack at another Nazi. Despite the odds, Peter seemed to have everything in hand. It was five against one, but he was managing.

But the fight was loud, and the noise carried out into the cafeteria. A couple seconds later, the entire Nazi meeting started to file into the kindergarten room. Peter backed up against a wall. Adesh pulled himself up onto a table.

It was a complete disaster. They were so going to die.

Even Peter couldn't take on fifty Nazis and survive.

There was a brief moment of peace and quiet as the other Nazis took stock of the situation. Then, they pounced.

Piper closed her eyes, willing it all to stop. There was an explosion, and Piper dropped to the ground. Her head throbbed, and she couldn't hear anything. She opened her eyes to see everyone else in the room on the floor, too.

But they recovered soon after enough to stand. But it was too late. Colonel Moshe Shaitrit and his three Mossad agents had entered through the windows after throwing in a concussion grenade. Armed only with knives, they got to work.

Adesh joined Piper, hiding against the wall, while Peter and the four Israelis formed a circle, standing back to back, as they took on Nazis one at a time.

"I was totally fine on my own," Peter yelled against the grunts and screams.

"Americans always think they're fine on their own, but they never are. You've watched too much John Wayne, Peter."

"No such thing as too much John Wayne," Peter said and punched a Nazi in the face.

"You should watch Israeli television," Moshe urged.

"Is there Israeli television?"

"No, we're too busy getting out and kicking ass to watch television."

"You and your Krav Maga bullshit. I spit on your Krav Maga bullshit," Peter said.

Two Nazis attacked him at once, but Moshe turned and kicked one of them in the liver, dropping him with one blow, so that Peter only had to fight one at a time.

"How's that for Krav Maga bullshit?" Moshe asked.

The fight ended in less than ten minutes. Most of the Nazis ran off, leaving a few of their compatriots on the floor.

But in all of the confusion, the blonds had escaped.

Piper checked the utility closet. It was filled with glue, construction paper, and crayons. But no Nazi scientist.

"Let's get out of here before the police come," Moshe commanded.

"Hold on. Let's check if they left something behind," Peter said.

Piper showed them utility closet and told them that Hans Schmidt had been held captive. The Israelis pulled out every piece of arts and crafts supplies, searching for clues, but there was nothing.

They were about to leave when Adesh pointed at a toy chest. "That looks weird," he said. "It's a toy chest, but it's bonded plastic. I'll bet it's lead-lined."

With the word *lead*, the air seemed to be sucked out of the room. Everyone froze in place. Lead was used to block radiation. Finally, Piper lifted the lid on the toy chest.

"These aren't toys," she said.

They all leaned over so they could look inside. "What is it?" Moshe asked.

"It's a lot of pieces. Metal and wires," Peter said.

"It's an atomic bomb," Piper said. "The pieces for it. At least most of it. The nuclear material isn't here."

"The crazy Nazis were building an atomic bomb in an elementary school," Adesh said.

"And they were using Hans Schmidt to do it," Peter said.

"They grabbed him out of Russia, and they're using him to build a bomb," Moshe said. "Oy vey. This is bad."

"This is bad," Peter repeated. "We have to save the Nazi from the Nazis before they explode the bomb and the Fourth Reich rises."

CHAPTER 13

There was nothing as nondescript and without charm as an Israeli government office. Dingy, white walls. Furniture that looked like it had been taken from a sixty-year-old public high school. No pictures on the wall. No rugs on the linoleum floors.

The Mossad were a lot like their offices. No frills. No nonsense. They were a group of extremely good-looking people who chain-smoked and had zero patience for bullshit.

They had brought Peter, Piper, Adesh, and the atomic bomb materials to Tel Aviv in a nondescript 747. Peter and Piper were put up in military housing in a tiny studio apartment, and Adesh was housed in an apartment a few doors down.

Peter and Piper slept like the dead. When they woke the next afternoon, they showered together and ate a delicious lunch in the mess hall. Adesh was nowhere to be found, but Peter wasn't too concerned. He felt safe with the Israelis. There was no way they would give him up to Nazis.

Moshe visited them at their table in the mess just as they were finishing lunch. "Debriefing meeting in an hour," he told Peter.

"I don't work for you. You can't debrief me."

"You wound me, Peter. Don't you want to play nice? Besides, we're going to debrief you. And your former bosses are coming, too."

That's how they all wound up in a too-cramped, institutional office. The Israelis and the Americans and Peter and Piper. The Israelis started the meeting by giving a rundown on Nazi groups around the world, none of whom concerned them at all, and none of whom were viable candidates for crazed Fourth Reich enthusiasts with an atomic bomb.

"We need to save the scientist before he builds those crazy bastards a bomb," Peter's old boss said. Peter shot him a death stare. If he had listened to Peter before, they wouldn't be in this mess. But to his credit, he was now including Peter and Piper in the plans. It was all hands on deck. They had even shared the information about the nuclear fuel with the Israelis in a desperate attempt to find it before it was too late.

"We've got all of our best tech guys following the chatter," Moshe told the meeting. "In addition, we've got Peter's man, who has been a huge boon to the mission in the past few hours."

So that's where Adesh was. He was playing with Israel's computer systems. Good for him. Maybe he could make peace in the Middle East while he was pushing buttons.

After about an hour, Adesh and a couple of Israelis came into the room and walked to the front. "We found him," Adesh announced. "He's in Berlin."

"That's sort of too much on the nose," Peter said. "I mean, it's not very creative on their part. Berlin? Couldn't the Nazis get a little creative? I hear Iceland's nice."

"Hans Schmidt must be happy to finally be returning home," Piper said. "I mean, except for the fact that he's being held prisoner and forced to build an atomic bomb."

"I guess we're all going to Berlin. Which safe house are we using?" Moshe asked.

The Israelis decided to stay at the Israeli safe house. The Americans decided to stay at the American safe house. And Peter and Piper decided on a five-star hotel in the center of town. Adesh was staying back in Tel Aviv to play with unlimited tech resources, and he was going to join them later.

Everyone was in their own place, but it was definitely a joint mission. Everyone was working together and sharing intel.

"I don't like it," Piper said, plopping down on the king-sized bed in their hotel suite. "Normally, we save the world on our own. Now, we have to save the world with two governments on our backs. We have to share."

"Sharing is caring," Peter said, searching through the mini fridge.

"And Adesh isn't here. It's like my right arm is gone without him. I like my right arm."

"I like your right arm, too. And your right hand with all of its fingers. How about you show me what your right hand can do right now?"

Peter took a soda out of the fridge and popped it open.

"My right hand is tired," Piper said. "It's been in five countries in the past few days. Besides, you had a big dose of my right hand on the plane."

Peter smirked. "That was the best plane ride I've

ever had. Emphasis on *ride*."

"I'm not sure we're supposed to have as much sex as we do. I think we're supposed to do other things to prove that we're in a stable relationship."

"You mean, like save the world? Fight with Nazis?" Peter asked.

"No, I mean like play Scrabble. Married people are always playing Scrabble in commercials. And they cook together. We've never cooked anything together."

"We've put lots of Pop-Tarts in the microwave for Adesh," Peter reminded her.

Piper thought of that for a moment. "I guess that counts. Okay, we can have sex again. But you're on top. And I want ice cream after."

"Mint chocolate chip?"

"And strawberry."

"Deal," he said and stripped out of his clothes. He was ready to go already. He was pretty much always ready for business. Like a 7-Eleven.

Piper stripped too, and lay on the bed, like an invitation. "Maybe we should stay naked all the time. It would save time."

"You don't have to tell me twice. I'm all for it."

Peter laid down on top of Piper, supporting his weight on his forearms, and nestled himself between her legs. She separated them further and then wrapped them around his waist. When he dragged his tongue over her breast and then the other, she arched her back to give him greater access. Her skin became alive, on fire and ice cold at the same time. Her flesh sprouted goosebumps, while her insides burned and throbbed.

"God, you're beautiful," Peter said. His voice brushed against her lips, making her shiver.

"I am when I'm with you," she moaned.

True to his word, he was on top. His hands grabbed her hips, and he entered her slowly, teasing her inch by inch. She was slick and ready for him, and she stretched naturally to accommodate him. Her pulse raced as he began to drive his body into her, and she felt her desire rise.

They touched each other eagerly, without breaking their connection. His rigid shaft inside her and the weight of his hard body on top of her all drove her to new heights. Her breath came faster as she neared her orgasm.

Peter raised her knees to enter her even deeper. He drove into her harder and faster. Her head fell back, and her eyes closed. She felt the rasp of his unshaven beard on her breast as his mouth found her nipple, sucking and kissing and heightening her sensations. They made love slowly, drawing out the moment for a long time.

"You're so wet. So ready," he breathed. "Piper. My Piper."

At the sound of her name spoken on his lips, so filled with emotion, her body clenched in ecstasy, unable to contain it any longer. Peter wasn't far behind. He groaned as he came, and after, he buried his face in her chest and kissed her, like he was thanking her over and over.

"You're welcome," she said, her voice choking with emotion.

Sex was great, but sex with Peter was on a whole different level. It was making love. Powerful, all-consuming love. If she wasn't careful, Piper would wind up absolutely lost in love with Peter, unable to ever get over it.

That would be awesome.

They fell asleep in each other's arms, but a few minutes later, Peter's phone rang, and he answered it. He spoke for only a couple of minutes and hung up.

"Gotta go," he said. "There's been a development. You rest, and I'll be right back."

"I'll come with you," she said with her eyes closed. She was dead tired, and even though she wanted to go with him and save the world, she couldn't bring herself to stay awake.

Peter got up and kissed the side of her head. "I

promise to call you if it gets life-threatening. I know how you enjoy getting almost killed."

"As long as you promise," she said and turned over. She heard him turn on the shower, and then she fell into a deep sleep.

She woke up about an hour later and bathed. The hotel offered a selection of luxury beauty products. She filled the bathtub and added lavender-scented bath salts. In the bath, she deep conditioned her hair and gave herself a facial. By the time she got out of the bathtub, she felt like a new woman. Pretty and well-rested and ready to track down Nazis and prevent an atomic bomb from going off.

She wrapped herself in a fluffy towel and studied herself in the mirror. At some point, she would need a haircut. Her red hair went down to her shoulder blades and got unruly during the day. Now, she pinned it up on her head. She opened a package with a red toothbrush in it, and just as she was about to put toothpaste on it, there was a noise in the other room.

"There you are!" she called through the closed door. "I'm still naked, so you're in luck, but if you didn't bring ice cream, I'm going to force you to stare at me naked and not do anything about it."

She listened for a response, but none came. That had never happened before. Peter was always ready with a snarky reply.

Piper froze in place. "Peter?" she called.

Nothing.

She opened the bathroom door slightly and saw two men dressed all in black with black ski masks over their heads and guns in their hands in the room. She slammed the door shut and locked it. She searched the bathroom in a panic for a weapon, but she couldn't find any. Peter hid weapons all over wherever he went, but she couldn't find one hidden in the towels.

She heard them approach, and her brain whirred into action. She pulled the hairdryer out of the wall by the door and tugged at the wires. In a blur, she wrapped the wires around the doorknob. She stood back and waited, sitting on the toilet.

"The toilet," she breathed. "Of course."

She opened the toilet tank and found a pistol with a silencer and an extra clip. She took them out and turned the safety off. One of the men touched the doorknob and let out a scream. There was a thud when she assumed he fell to the floor, electrocuted.

A man cursed in German, and a muffled shot rang out. He must have had a silencer, too. There was a large hole in the door, and the bullet had just missed her and lodged in the wall above her head.

"I refuse to die in the bathroom," she said and

shot at the door, emptying the gun. When she was done, she hopped into the bathtub and waited for more shooting.

But nothing happened.

Nothing until she heard the suite's door open, and heavy footsteps come close.

"Piper? Piper!" she heard Peter cry. She had never heard so much fear in his voice. He was completely panicked.

"In here," she called. "But don't touch the doorknob!"

"Stand back!" he ordered. There was a loud noise, and what remained of the door broke open. It slammed against the wall and fell off the hinges. Peter stepped into the bathroom. His eyes were wild, and his face was white as a sheet. When he saw Piper in the tub, a tear rolled down his cheek. He sprinted to her and picked her up and hugged her to his large frame.

"I saw the bodies, and I thought I had lost you," he breathed. "I couldn't survive that. Do you hear me? I can't lose you."

"You won't lose me," she whispered. "If I'm about to die, I promise to take you with me."

Peter put her down. "What if you can't kill me? I'm pretty indestructible. I've been trained to be tough and survive practically anything."

"Don't worry. I'll figure out a way to kill you. I promise."

"Deal," he said. She wiped the tears from his cheek and kissed him lightly.

Moshe stuck his head into the bathroom. "Everything all right?"

"Yes. They tried to kill me," she told him.

They stepped back into the living room. Moshe had brought two Israeli agents with him. They had taken the ski masks off of the intruders. They all studied their faces.

"Nazis?" Moshe asked Peter.

He shrugged. "Never seen them before."

A creepy feeling went up Piper's spine. "I know them," she said.

"You do?" Peter asked.

"I know them, but I don't know who they are and I don't know how I know them or where I've seen them before."

"Is that code?" Moshe asked.

Piper dropped to the floor and rifled through one of the men's pockets. She pulled out a photo. It was a picture of her. In it, her hair was shorter, but she looked the same age. She was wearing a blue sweatshirt and no makeup.

Piper continued to study the photo for clues to

her identity. These men were after her. They knew her, and they wanted her dead. No one had tried to kill her for weeks, but the danger continued. There was something about her that was dangerous, something that needed to be snuffed out.

"Can you deal with the bodies quietly?" Peter asked Moshe. "And we'd appreciate if you could find out what you can about them and tell us what you find."

"Is this a personal thing? Off the clock?" Moshe asked.

Peter nodded. "Off the clock. A favor. I'll owe you one."

Moshe smiled. It was obvious that he liked the sound of an owed favor.

They whisked the bodies away, and Peter sat on the couch with Piper after he handed her a mini bottle of booze to calm her nerves.

"This is me," she said, showing him the photo.

"I recognize the twinkly eyes and the come hither look."

"I think I look hardened. Angry," she said, studying the picture.

"That makes sense. You hadn't met me yet. I turned you into the beautiful woman you are. I deserve all the credit."

He was joking, but she wondered if it was true.

Maybe she was someone she didn't like. Maybe what made her whole was Peter.

Piper put her head on Peter's shoulder and breathed in the scent of his cologne. "This is nice," she said. "You and me."

"And the aftermath of near death. By the way, it was ingenious of you to rig the doorknob."

"Thank you for hiding a gun in the toilet. That came in handy."

"Some men bring flowers, but I think that's old hat," he said.

Piper looked at the photo again, but her attackers' faces flashed in her mind. "This is going to sound crazy, but I can't help but have the feeling that those two men were family."

"You mean they were brothers? They didn't look much alike, but you never know."

"No," she said. "My family. I don't know why, but I think they were my family."

"That would be a bummer. My brother and I have had our share of fights, but Spencer never tried to shoot me. Seriously, though, the Israelis will do a full genetic test on them. If anyone can get information out of a corpse, it's the Israelis. We should have information soon."

"Thank you," she said, snuggling up to him in

her towel.

"It's not me. Moshe is thorough."

"No, I mean thank you for everything. For loving me."

"Oh, that. That's totally out of my control. Like blinking or farting in my sleep."

CHAPTER 14

"We're looking for a one-legged man?" Piper asked.

"He's got a prosthetic, so officially, he has two legs," Peter said. "But one of them is detachable."

"And the one-legged man is the key?"

Yes, the one-legged man was the key. Adesh had done his job and saved the day. He had found that the one-legged man in Berlin was talking a lot about Hans Schmidt. He knew where he was, and if they tracked down the one-legged man, they could find the scientist, the Nazis, and the nuclear fuel.

"Yes, he's the key to saving the world," Peter said.

He squeezed Piper's hand. If he were honest with himself, his heart wasn't in capturing the one-legged man and saving the world. He had almost lost Piper, and now all he wanted to do was spend every second with her, return to San Francisco with her, and wear khaki Dockers.

Peter's former boss had called him in on the arrest. It was the agency's idea of being magnanimous, but Peter knew it was a way of showing him just how powerful and successful they were. For all intents and purposes, they had broken a terrifying conspiracy without shedding any blood, and they wanted Peter as a witness, like Roger Federer playing in front of a crowd at Wimbledon.

Peter and Piper met the Americans and the Israelis outside of the one-legged man's residence, but they weren't going to be involved in taking him down. They were instructed to stay out of harm's way next door while the Americans stormed the apartment and the Israelis were used as backup downstairs. They weren't needed. The one-legged man was captured without incident, a black hood was put over his head, and he was moved into American custody, rushed away in an unmarked van without anyone taking notice.

"Piece of cake," Peter's former boss told him. "Thanks for your help. We'll be taking it from here."

"But you need us," Piper said.

"No, we don't."

"We know what the Nazis look like. We've seen Hans Schmidt," she continued, trying to convince him. It was no use. He dismissed her like she wasn't important and had nothing to offer.

"We'll interrogate our man, and this will be wrapped up by the end of the day."

Moshe shrugged, agreeing with Peter's former boss. "Sorry, Peter. It was fun, but it's time to move on."

"But…" Piper started.

Peter wrapped his arm around her shoulders. "It's over. This adventure's done. We saved the world."

"But there wasn't a shoot-out. No explosions," Piper complained, her face the picture of disappointment.

"You win some. You lose some."

It was a hard pill for Piper to swallow, but Peter finally convinced her to let it go. They walked back to the hotel and were happy to find Adesh waiting for them in the lobby. He was laden down with computer bags and smiled when he saw them.

"Did you find the atomic bomb?" he asked.

"No, but the powers that be found it," Peter said.

"They took over the mission. They told us to go home," Piper grumbled.

"Good idea," Adesh said. "I stole a lot of intel from the Israelis, so it's probably a good idea to get back to the States as soon as possible."

"I agree. Probably a good idea," Peter said.

"I guess we'll have to save the world another day," Piper said.

"I've been hearing good things about schnitzel. Can we grab some fast before we leave?" Adesh asked.

The three shared a meal at the best schnitzel restaurant in Berlin, which was a tiny dive in a rundown area. It had four small tables and one surly waiter who was the son of the owner and definitely didn't want to be there.

The ambiance may have lacked a certain something, but the food was delicious. Still, the three of them picked at their food slowly. They had helped the authorities squelch a Nazi conspiracy and had prevented the construction and detonation of an atomic bomb. So, it should have been a celebratory meal.

Instead, they were a somber group after a disappointing outcome. In the end, they had only been third-party observers. Contractors.

Sidekicks.

It had finally happened to Peter, his most dreaded fear. He had become a sidekick. The superheroes had captured the one-legged man who was going to lead them to the blonds and the nuclear fuel. Meanwhile, Peter, Piper, and Adesh were just eating fried meat.

Peter was in a sidekick funk. He wondered if Robin had felt this way, living with Batman for all of those years.

"Holy Nazis, Batman," Peter muttered.

"What?" Piper asked, picking at her food with her fork.

"Maybe this is for the best," Peter said. "Now we have time to figure out about those dead guys and how they were your family."

"That sounds great," Piper said, like it wasn't great at all.

"We might finally have a lead on discovering who you are," Peter continued.

"Swell," she said. "Family that wants me dead. Maybe it's better being an orphan."

"Are you sure about the one-legged man?" Peter asked Adesh. "Are you sure he was the linchpin to the whole thing?"

"Funny you should ask. I've been thinking about him. He was so easy to find, when I couldn't find a thing about the blond Nazis. It was almost like… No, forget it."

Piper pushed her plate aside and leaned forward. "Like what?" she asked.

"Like Hansel and Gretel's breadcrumbs. Like the trail was left for me. It was easy to find. Easy to follow.

Easier than finding Gal Gadot's home address, I can tell you."

"Batman wouldn't take this lying down," Peter said. He closed his eyes and tried to think straight. What wasn't he seeing? Again, he was struck by the idea that this was all smoke and mirrors. Sleight of hand. A cheap Vegas magic trick. They were looking right, but maybe they were supposed to look left.

"I guess we'll never know," he said, and speared a piece of schnitzel.

Their waiter turned on a small television on the counter and began to flip through the stations. "No football games," he complained to them. "The stupid G7 meeting is taking up all of the television."

He was about to turn off the TV, but Peter stopped him. On the screen, he watched the news report about the arrival of heads of state for the meeting that gathered the seven richest countries on the planet. The leaders were going to be gathering in a few hours for their opening meeting.

"I'm so stupid," Peter said. "I'm Robin stupid. No wonder I'm a sidekick. I don't deserve to be Batman. The caped crusader would never allow himself to be hoodwinked like this."

"Like what? Like what?" Piper asked. Her eyes searched the restaurant, probably trying to find what had set Peter off. Then, her eyes locked onto the television screen. Peter watched as her mouth opened slowly, as realization dawned.

"The G7," she breathed.

"The perfect target," Peter noted.

"What? What's happening?" Adesh asked.

"When does the meeting start?" Peter asked the waiter.

"Three hours. The traffic is locked up in the city until then," the waiter answered.

In order to dot all the I's and cross all the T's, Peter contacted his boss and the Israelis. He told them about the G7, about it being the perfect target. But who listens to Robin? Peter was told that the one-legged man had been a minefield. He had told them about a neo-Nazi group who had the nuclear fuel and the scientist in Venezuela and were planning on using it to set off a bomb in New York City. No amount of arguing would convince them.

"Venezuela. New York City. The one-legged man told them everything they wanted to know. Everything they wanted to hear, more like it," Peter said.

"So, it's up to us?" Piper asked, excited. "Tell me it's up to us."

"The team's getting back together?" Adesh asked, full of hope.

Peter nodded. "We're going to have to save the world again. If we don't, we'll probably be incinerated in a nuclear mushroom cloud. Our faces will melt off, and our bones will turn to dust. But I hear it only hurts for a second."

"That's comforting," Piper said.

"If we're going to get nuked, I'm going to finish my schnitzel," Adesh said. "Can I get dessert, too? I have a glandular problem. Dessert will help my energy level, and we might need it to save the world again."

The waiter had been right about the traffic, so they walked to the G7 meeting. Security was off the charts, and they couldn't get within a block of the building.

"But people still have to come and go," Peter noted. "It's a big gathering. They have to eat, drink, and crap. They need people."

"I can make us people with whatever credentials you want," Adesh offered. "What kind of people should we be?"

Piper pointed to a caterer's van that passed through security into the building's underground parking structure without a problem. "How about servers? That would get us close."

CHAPTER 15

Peter was staring at Piper's boobs.

"Stop staring at my boobs," Piper said.

"I'm not staring at your boobs."

"I could draw a direct line from your eyeballs to my breasts. You haven't even blinked. I can see the reflection of my boobs on your irises."

Peter blinked. "Maybe I was looking at your boobs, but it's hard not to."

"It's this damned server's shirt. It must belong to a flat-chested woman. I can't button it." She tugged at the white fabric, trying to get the buttons closer to the buttonholes, but it was no use. In the too small shirt and the miniskirt, she looked like the first five minutes of a porn movie.

"I wasn't looking at your boobs," Adesh said. "I was trying to get my pants on."

It was a hopeless task. He had decided to keep his t-shirt on and put the uniform's shirt over it without buttoning it. Still, the arms and the back had ripped. As for the pants, there was no way they were going to make it up over his hips.

"My uniform fits perfectly," Peter said. It was true. Everything buttoned up without a problem, but his pants were six inches too short and so were his shirtsleeves.

"This might not work," Piper said, taking stock of how they looked. "We're not exactly inconspicuous."

"It's fine. We're not looking for a promotion. We're just scoping out Nazis so they don't set off an atomic weapon at an international governmental meeting," Peter said.

They had stolen the uniforms from the caterer's van while Adesh had hacked into the G7's event planner's computer system so that he could make them badges. They had gotten dressed in a Pizza Hut bathroom across the street, and now they walked to the G7 building, hoping the badges were enough to get them through, even though they looked ridiculous in the uniforms that didn't fit.

"If they give us any trouble, flash your boobs,"

Peter told Piper.

"I don't need to flash anything. They're like neon signs without me doing a thing."

It turned out that no one looked twice at them. Adesh's badges did the trick. They were allowed in, and as soon as they entered, the catering company put them to work. They were happy for more bodies to help with serving in the massive event.

The G7 leaders were enjoying a pre-meeting mixer party with drinks and appetizers. Peter was handed a platter of stuffed mushroom caps to serve. Piper was given a platter of mini-Cuban sandwiches, and Adesh was given a platter of crystal glasses filled with champagne.

"I'm not sure I should carry this," Adesh told the catering manager. "Sometimes I lose my balance when I'm under pressure."

"Get in there. France is a bitch if she doesn't get her booze," the manager told him.

"But…" he started, but the manager waved him off.

Adesh followed Peter and Piper into the ballroom. He put one of his arms out straight at his side to better balance himself, but Piper could hear the clinking of the wine glasses as he walked.

"I'm going to drop champagne on world leaders and start a world war," Adesh said.

"Just remember why we're here," Peter said. "We need to track down the blond Nazis. Find the scientist. Stop the bomb."

"Okay," Adesh said. There was sweat streaming down his face. "I'm used to working from home. I have social anxiety."

"You're not being social. You're hunting prey," Peter said.

"You're saving the world," Piper added.

"Oh, that's right," Adesh said. "I guess that's not very social."

"Keep your eyes peeled, team. Time is of the essence. We could be vaporized at any second," Peter said.

Piper recognized a lot of the faces. It was impressive to see so much power in one room. The prime minister of Italy took three of Piper's mini Cuban sandwiches and winked at her boobs. She tried not to get distracted by the high-profile people and refocused on finding the blonds. Unfortunately, there were a lot of blonds.

Each time she saw a blond head, she would start heading in their direction, but it was never one of the Nazis. Peter was working the edges of the party, and Adesh was saying sorry to the Chinese premier for spilling a glass of champagne on him.

It dawned on Piper that the bomb didn't need to be at the meeting. It was an atomic bomb. It could have been placed anywhere in Berlin, and it would have served the same purpose. If that was the case, they would never find the bomb. It was a waste of time. A tragedy was about to happen, and there was nothing they could do about it.

She searched for Peter to tell him that they had messed up, but he had disappeared into the crowd with his stuffed mushroom caps. She put her platter down on a nearby table and walked around the perimeter of the room.

Halfway around, she found him.

Not Peter.

Hans Schmidt, the Nazi scientist.

She had found the man who had been abducted by Nazis to build them an atomic bomb. He was standing in a corner by a door. His eyes were darting back and forth, like he was afraid.

The blond Nazis must have left him alone for a minute. It was Piper's chance to save him. She sprinted over to him, desperate to reach him before his handlers returned.

She practically tackled the scientist. "Come with me if you want to live," she said, startling him. She opened the side door and pushed him through. She found a small office down the hall, and they went inside. She locked the door and barred it with a desk. Then, she called Peter and Adesh and told them to meet her there.

A couple of minutes later, they were all together in the locked room, staring at the elderly scientist, who was sitting on a desk chair, studying his hands.

Despite his age, he was a handsome man. Trim with a nice head of thick white hair.

"You're saved," Piper said.

He looked up at her and rubbed his eyes, as if he was trying to focus. "I am?"

"Yes," Peter said.

"It's been so long. The Russians took me in forty-five, and then these madmen took me days ago."

He stood and hugged Piper. "Thank you."

He shook on his feet, so they helped him sit, again. "What happened? Everyone thought you were dead again in Russia," Adesh asked.

"Madmen. Crazy men," Hans Schmidt started, shaking his head. "I was working in my laboratory when they stormed the facility. It was a national holiday, so most of the staff was drunk in the cafeteria. They didn't know what was happening until too late.

"They threatened me at gunpoint, and they forced me to extract the nuclear material. I'm so ashamed, but please understand me. I had been held prisoner for many decades. I had learned how to survive. Survival governed me. So, I did what the lunatics told me to."

Piper gnawed on her lower lip. Her memory was gone, but that didn't change the fact that she had been abducted too. And tortured. What had she agreed to do under duress? Had she remained strong or cracked under pressure in order to survive? She had most likely been held captive for a relatively short time, unlike Hans Schmidt.

After decades in captivity, he was probably a completely different man than he was as a young Nazi scientist in Berlin. He had to be a broken shell, a mere shadow of who he used to be. His dark past had melted away, as far as Piper was concerned. It looked like Peter and Adesh were feeling the same way.

"Understandable," Peter said. "How did the accident happen?"

"They made me do that, too, with a timed charge that went off when they had secreted me away. At first, I thought I was finally free. Yes, they had stolen nuclear fuel, but I was out of Russia, free of the Soviet Union once and for all. I cried at my freedom. You know, I was never a Nazi. Never."

"That's not true," Peter said. "We've seen your records."

"Let me explain. At that time, everyone was a

Nazi. We had no choice in the matter. Maybe I learned the art of survival at a very young age. And I was young. I was the youngest scientist in the nuclear program during the war. I loved science. Lived for science. But as God is my witness, I never shared their philosophy. I never hated the Jewish people. In fact, one of my best friends in school was a Jew. He was a very good man. I swear to God, I've never done any wrong to the Jewish people."

Out of the corner of Piper's eye, she saw Peter flinch slightly. Adesh was crying freely and wiped his eyes with the back of his hand.

"So, they took you out of Russia and went to Italy," Peter said. "Why? What was the jewelry museum about?"

"Huh?" the scientist said. "Oh, that. It was silly. They wanted me to do their dirty deeds so they tried to make me happy."

"Oh, so they were going to give you jewelry?" Adesh asked.

"No. Well, yes," the scientist said. "It was my jewelry. My family's jewelry."

"Excuse me?" Peter asked.

"My family had an extensive jewelry collection, passed down from generation to generation. It was all stolen from us. It meant a lot to me, and these crazy Nazis knew it."

"Where's the jewelry now?" Piper asked.

"They took it back when I did what they wanted."

"Dammit," Peter said. "You did what they wanted. So, it's done. You made the bomb."

"An atomic bomb? You made an atomic bomb?" Adesh asked.

"I had no choice. They are crazy. Crazy!" Hans's voice rose and cracked. He started to cough. Piper took a carafe of water off of one of the desks and poured a glass for him. Hans drank it down and wiped his mouth.

"How crazy are they? Give me specifics," Peter said.

"They're Nazis. Isn't that crazy enough?" Hans said.

"No. I need to know specifics. What's the bomb for? What are their plans?" Peter insisted. Piper recognized that voice. It was Peter's serious voice.

"They're mad," Hans continued. "They want to create the Fourth Reich. Don't they know that Germany is the richest country in Europe? It's already won. But they want more. They want destruction. They want war."

Peter shook his head. "They want to rebuild what was. They don't care how rich and well-off Germany is. They want to revive the past."

"Exactly," Hans said. "Crazy men. Crazy! And how they're going to do it? Terrible. We are all about to die."

Adesh sat down on a chair. "I don't want to die. How soon are we talking about?"

"Where's the bomb?" Piper asked. She held her breath, waiting for the answer and hoping that he wouldn't say it was out of reach and impossible to stop.

"Oh, the bomb," Hans said.

"Where's the bomb?" Peter yelled, losing all patience. "Tell us now!"

Hans didn't flinch. He must have been used to being yelled at. He had spent most of his long life as a prisoner.

"It's here. There are a series of tunnels under the building. It's set to go off just as the meeting begins."

"That's crazy," Piper said, incredulous. "That will destroy Berlin. The country probably won't survive, either."

"They don't care," Hans said. "They want to make a big statement, taking the seven leaders down and erasing the new Deutschland in order to start fresh with the Fourth Reich."

"And they left you here to die?" Adesh asked.

"That's not important right now," Peter said. "Can you defuse the bomb?"

"Of course, but I don't know if there's time," Hans said.

Peter grabbed the old man by the arm and pulled him up. "You'll do it in time. Now, show us where it is."

CHAPTER 16

"You're being a little rough with him," Piper whispered to Peter as they followed Hans through the underground tunnels to find and defuse the atomic bomb.

"He's a Nazi. He built an atomic bomb for Nazis. There's literally a ticking time bomb until we die."

"He *was* a Nazi. He's been through a lot. He was held prisoner for most of his life. That's a lot to go through." Piper's voice broke, and she hated herself for it. She wished she could get over her abduction. After all, she didn't remember it, only her escape. She shouldn't have been traumatized. She should have adapted and gotten over the whole thing. Peter would have gotten over it. He had almost died a million times in his career.

Peter took her hand and brought it to his lips, kissing it. "I'm sorry. I'll be nicer to the Nazi scientist while he takes us to the atomic weapon he built to blow up Berlin."

Peter pulled a gun out of his waistband. He had to leave his ankle holster behind at Pizza Hut because his ankles were visible in his too-short uniform. "I've got a bad feeling, though," Peter said.

"Like we're going to be vaporized, and I'll never make sweet love to Lola Franklin?" Adesh asked, worried.

"No, like the blond Nazis are going to notice that their captive has vanished, and they're on their way to find him."

"That's not bad," Adesh said. "You can handle a bunch of blond Nazis."

"Thanks for your confidence," Peter said. "I'd be happier if you brought a bazooka. You didn't, did you?"

"I'm more or less a pacifist," Adesh said. "Unless it's a cyberwar. I've done a few of those."

"The blonds are probably long gone," Piper told Peter. "They'd want to be outside of the mushroom cloud and save themselves so they can start the Fourth Reich."

"Smart. Of course," Peter said.

The tunnels were a crisscross maze that led deep beneath Berlin. Piper had visions of Hitler's bunker and wondered if she was walking near it.

"My spine's tingling," Piper said.

"I'm getting claustrophobia," Adesh said. "This place is spooky."

"Just a little bit this way," Hans called. "We're almost there."

Peter stopped walking. "Do you hear that?"

Piper stopped, too, and listened. "It's the pipes. There're a lot of pipes. That's what we're hearing."

"It sounds like the buffalo stampede," Adesh said and hugged himself. "Do they keep buffalo down here? I don't want to do the buffalo thing again. That was bad. I still have nightmares about hooves."

"Uh-oh," Peter said and raised his gun. "It's not buffalo. I think it's something much worse. Grab something. Find a weapon."

Adesh and Piper looked around for something. Anything. Adesh grabbed hold of some pipe and pulled hard. A three-foot section came away in his hand. Piper found a large rock on the floor and picked it up.

"Ready!" Piper yelled.

Hans dropped to the floor and rolled into a corner, hiding. The sound of a buffalo stampede grew louder and closer.

And then, they were on them.

Not buffalo.

Blond Nazis.

Lots and lots of blond Nazis.

"Don't let them take me again," Hans cried. "Please let me be free!"

"We've got you surrounded!" Piper yelled at the blonds. "Freeze in the name of the law!"

Peter shot her a look. "Very official. Very commanding. I might be turned on, Piper."

One of the Nazis shot his gun, and the bullet ricocheted off the stone walls. Everyone dropped to the floor and waited for the bullet to stop its zigzag trajectory. It was a brief moment of calm before the Nazis would kill them, Piper thought.

She knew Peter would put up a good fight, but it would be impossible to win. There were too many Nazis.

Maybe that's why Peter shot first before anyone got back up. He picked off what looked like the lead Nazi while he was on the floor. Then Peter bounded up and flew through the air, cold-cocked two other Nazis, and shot another.

Four down.

A million more Nazis to go.

Adesh let out a rebel yell. He swung his piece of pipe over his head and struggled to get up off of his belly. The Nazis turned their attention to him. One of them pointed his gun directly at Adesh, but Piper threw her rock and hit the gun out of his hand. She dove for the gun, which had fallen onto the floor. She managed to grab it, but the Nazi was lunging for it, too, and he tried to get it out of her hands.

He was stronger than she was, but she refused to be killed by a Nazi. She wanted to live a happy life with Peter, and she wasn't going to let a racist, narcissistic, megalomaniac ruin that. She kicked at the Nazi, but he grabbed hold of the gun's barrel and pulled. He was going to get the gun! She held tight to it. Tighter. Tighter.

The gun went off in her hand. The Nazi grunted and rolled off her. Piper's hand stayed clenched, and the gun went off again.

And again.

And again, and again, and again, and again.

A whole lot of agains.

When she finally stopped shooting, six more Nazis lay dead, shot full of lead. Piper sat up and looked in shock at the destruction she had wrought.

Behind her, Adesh finally managed to get off the floor. He wielded the pipe and started swinging it and running at some of the few Nazis who were still alive. Peter had dispatched a few more, like he was James Bond and Bruce Lee wrapped into one hot guy. He alternated between shooting, martial arts, and bar brawling. The remaining two Nazis ran in horror from Adesh's length of pipe and his impressive girth.

Peter, Piper, and Adesh watched them flee and then looked down at the dead Nazis at their feet as they tried to catch their breath.

Somehow, the three had survived. They had vanquished the horde of Nazis. Peter checked on Piper, and then he turned to Hans Schmidt, who was cowering in a corner, terrified.

"The bomb, Doctor. The bomb," Peter urged.

Peter helped Hans up. "We must hurry!" Hans said. "We don't have much time until it goes off. Please, let us hurry." He grabbed Peter's shoulders and stared into his eyes. "Finally, in my life, I'm on the side of good. I'm on the right side. I need to help you. I need to make this up to the world. I need to be a hero."

Peter smiled at him, and Piper assumed that at that very moment, Peter bonded with Hans Schmidt. If Peter understood one thing, it was the drive to be a hero.

"Let's go," he said.

Hans ran as fast as he could, and Peter, Piper, and Adesh ran after him toward the bomb. Left, right, right, left, down, down, they ran through the twisting and turning tunnels. Finally, Hans stopped in front of a tiny door, only a couple of feet high.

"It's in here," he said. "There's only room for one. I'll defuse the bomb. You all leave and get as far away as you can."

"We can't leave you alone. That's not right," Piper told him, touched by his selfless courage.

"Go now. There's only room for one in there. I'll handle the bomb. Let me do this. I want to do right in the world."

Piper hugged him, and Peter shook his hand. They watched the scientist squeeze through the tiny door, and close it behind him. The three turned around and walked back through the tunnel.

"I didn't know Nazis could be such nice people," Adesh said, as they walked away. "I mean, he's going to save the world and possibly sacrifice himself. That's a really nice Nazi."

Peter stopped walking. "A nice Nazi," he said, like he was tasting the words in his mouth.

"A nice Nazi," Piper repeated. "It sounds like an oxymoron to me."

"Who's a moron?" Adesh asked.

"Us," Peter said. "We got hoodwinked. There's no such thing as a nice Nazi."

Peter ran full out down the tunnel toward the tiny door, and Piper followed him. The door was locked, but Peter kicked it open. He squeezed through on his stomach, and Piper went in after. Adesh stayed in the tunnel and waited for them because he couldn't fit through the door.

The door didn't lead to a room. It led to another tunnel. There was no sign of an atomic bomb. No sign of anything kept there.

But they could hear Hans's footsteps in the distance. He had run away, but he hadn't gotten far.

Peter took his gun out of his waistband and ran toward the sound. Piper ran after him.

"Stop, or I'll shoot!" Peter yelled ahead of her. "I mean it, Nazi. I'll kill you."

Piper caught up with them. Hans turned around and smiled weakly at Peter. "Thank goodness you're here. They must have moved the bomb. I was just looking for it."

"Stop lying," Peter sneered.

"I'm not lying. Those men are crazy. They had me make them a bomb, and then they hid it so that I couldn't defuse it. That has to be what happened. Don't you see? Don't you see?"

Hans waved his arms wildly while he spoke. He was desperate to be believed. Probably because he was a liar.

"You're a liar," Piper said.

"No! I'm not lying. Listen, we don't have time to talk right now. We need to find that bomb. I'm the only one who can stop it from killing millions!"

"You're a good liar, but you're a liar," Piper said.

"Not such a good liar," Peter said. "I knew it before, but I didn't trust my own judgment. 'As God is my witness.' he said. 'I swear to God' he said. Those are tells. Guilty men say that. Everyone learns that in interrogation 101. It's basic."

"I didn't lie!" Hans insisted. "We need to hurry. Please, you can believe me or not, but we need to take care of the bomb!"

"That's why you flinched," Piper said to Peter. "It hit you wrong when he was talking about how much he loved Jews. There was something else that hit me wrong about it. Why would he talk so much about Jews? We hadn't been talking about Jews. But we had been talking about…"

"The jewelry," Peter said and laughed.

"No provenance!" Peter and Piper exclaimed in union.

"The jewelry in Rome had no provenance. It wasn't because it was your family's jewelry," Piper said to Hans. "It was because it had been stolen from Jews during the war. How many works of art and valuables had been stolen from persecuted Jews? Too many to count. You stole that jewelry. You stole it from murdered Jews. Deny it. Go on. I dare you to deny it."

Hans reached behind him and pulled a gun out of his waistband, aiming it at Peter's head. "Why would

I deny it? I'm proud of it."

CHAPTER 17

Peter and Hans were at a standoff. Each of them held a gun in their outstretched hands. Each pointed their weapon at the other's head. Piper expected them to fire at any second, but they stood without moving a muscle.

Hans Schmidt's face had transformed. Gone was the traumatized old man. Gone was the innocent, who had been held prisoner for the majority of his life.

In his place was a vicious, evil Nazi. Without much imagination, Piper could picture him in his uniform so many years ago.

"We were princes," Hans began with a snide smile. "All of us. Princes among mere peasants. Princes for a genius, all-powerful king. They've never made uniforms like that since. We were godlike in them."

"Godlike. Princes. You're mixing your metaphors," Peter said.

"Americans and their stupid humor," Hans sneered. "We had almost conquered the entire world. You shouldn't have fought us. Can you imagine the world if we had won? It would be free of Jewish filth."

"And the trains would run on time. Yada. Yada. I know. Get on with it," Peter said.

"I lived in a beautiful apartment not far from here. Four bedrooms. It even had a ballroom," Hans continued. He seemed determined to tell his story.

"A stolen apartment. Stolen from Jews I'd bet," Piper said.

"The Jews had stolen it before me! Vermin who lied, cheated, and stole. We were cleaning the world from their filth."

"Why haven't I shot him yet?" Peter asked Piper. "I should have shot him, already. I really, really want him to die."

"In a moment, we're all going to die," Hans said with a smile.

"It was all your idea," Piper said, understanding. "You were obsessed with your glamorous Nazi life before the Soviets had captured you and forced you to work for them. Then, one day you saw on the internet about the jewelry exhibit in Rome. Your ill-gotten goods. Your ties to the good old days."

"So, you contacted a bunch of crazy fanatics," Peter said, catching on. "You organized the whole thing from captivity. But how? If you could do all that, why didn't you escape?"

"I did escape. Remember?" Hans said. "But I wanted to escape *big*."

"The Fourth Reich was your idea. All of it was your idea. You blew it all up in Russia, and you managed to steal your stolen jewelry. Neat and tidy," Piper said.

"Why are you surprised? I'm a genius scientist. I can figure out how to create the Fourth Reich."

"You're crazy," Piper said.

"Crazy enough to do this!" Hans yelled and pulled the trigger.

Civilians were idiots when it came to guns. Even gun enthusiasts were boneheads. Peter had seen more than one bonehead stick his eyeball against the barrel of a gun to see if it was dirty.

And in times like these, in the heat of the battle, when people had gotten killed and everything was on the line, civilians—even those trained by the Nazi military during World War Two—never ever checked their gun.

Never.

But Peter wasn't a civilian. He wasn't a gun enthusiast.

He was a badass superspy, and that's why he knew that the gun that Nazi scientist Hans Schmidt was aiming at Peter's head wasn't loaded. He knew that because it was Peter's gun, and Peter had emptied its bullets into the bodies of a bunch of blond Nazis. Once it had been emptied, he had gotten rid of it and picked up one of the dead Nazi's guns, and he was aiming that one at Hans's head.

And it was loaded.

Hans must have found Peter's empty gun on the floor and taken it during the action. He was cocksure that he was about to blow away Peter, and Peter wanted to give him his little moment of victory, but time was ticking away, and Peter needed to move things along.

Hans decided to move things along, too. Without saying another word, he pulled the trigger to shoot Peter in the head. But nothing happened, just as Peter knew it would. The gun wasn't loaded.

Hans's mouth dropped open in honest shock. He pulled the trigger more times, but it didn't fire. Peter lowered his gun and doubled over in laughter.

"He thought the gun was loaded!" Peter roared

with laughter. "He aimed it at my head and blathered on and on. 'I'm a Nazi.' 'I'm Hitler's prince.' What a dweeb."

"Yes, it's funny," Piper said. "But remember there's an atomic bomb ready to go off. If I'm vaporized, I can never fondle your you-know-what again."

Peter stopped laughing and wiped his eyes. He grew serious. "We wouldn't want that. Where's the bomb, Nazi? Speak up, or I'll Eichmann your ass."

"I'll never tell!" Hans yelled and threw the gun at Peter. Peter dodged it easily. "You'll never find it! Never."

Hans turned around and began to run. Peter looked at Piper and sighed heavily. "He thinks he's going to outrun me," he said, sadly. "I'm a patient man, but come on."

Peter was about to chase after him, when Hans tripped and went down hard. Peter and Piper went to help him up, but Hans had hit his head. He was lying in a puddle of his own blood, and he wasn't breathing.

"That's unfortunate, considering we don't know where the bomb is," Peter said, looking at Hans's lifeless body.

"Is that a room up ahead?" Piper asked.

Peter squinted into the tunnel. There was a little light coming from a doorway. "It can't be that easy."

"You know what? I bet he told us the truth,"

Piper said. "He wasn't going to defuse the bomb, but he wasn't lying about where it was. He said the bomb was through the tiny door, and it was. It's just a little way up there."

Peter wrapped his arms around Piper and hugged her. "My sweet, darling Piper. It can't be that easy. It's never that easy. And Nazis are notorious liars."

Piper pulled away from him. "Follow me."

They followed the light to an open doorway. They walked through to a large, empty room.

Empty except for an atomic bomb.

"Holy shit, it's real," Peter breathed. "A part of me thought it was all a lie and there was no atomic bomb. I can't believe how crazy people are. Have you noticed how crazy people are?"

Piper pointed at the bomb. "Can we talk about the state of the world after we take care of the bomb?"

They approached the bomb on tiptoes, careful not to make any sudden movements. The bomb had a large countdown clock on it.

"Two minutes," Peter read. "Of course."

"Defuse it," Piper told him. "Stop the clock and dismantle the bomb."

"Uh…" Peter said.

"Go ahead. Hurry up. The seconds aren't getting slower."

"The thing is that I don't know how to dismantle an atomic bomb. I've never seen one. This is way above my pay grade. I have no clue what to do. Do you still love me?"

Piper kissed him lightly on the lips. "Love you to the moon and back. Of course, we might actually be blown to the moon in a few seconds, so I guess I'll have to defuse it."

"You know how to do that?" Peter asked, surprised.

"You know what? I think I do."

CHAPTER 18

The G7 went without a hitch, despite the dead Nazis and atomic bomb beneath it. Afterwards, the Germans made a stink that an atomic bomb was set to blow up Berlin and the Americans didn't warn them. It was a giant diplomatic hiccough.

But that's what Peter and Piper were told later on because they skipped town immediately after dismantling the bomb. With their mission done, they contacted Peter's former boss and caught him up. Then, they drove directly to the private airport with Adesh and took a private plane back to San Francisco.

Halfway there, Adesh cried out while he was on his laptop. "She messaged back! She messaged back!"

"Who?" Peter asked.

"Lola Franklin. She wants to go out with me. At least I think she does. What's goat yoga?"

Peter fist-bumped Adesh. "You're in, bro! You bagged Lola Franklin!"

"What should I wear to goat yoga? I'm thinking something she'll never forget. I have a kickass Darth Maul costume."

Peter decided to let Adesh plan on dressing like Darth Maul, and when the time came, Peter would set him straight so he wouldn't scare off Lola.

Adesh was continuing to message with Lola when the Israelis called Peter. He took notes from the call and hung up after a few minutes.

"Are you sitting down?" he asked Piper.

"No, I'm lying down," she said. "You can see me, can't you? Should I worry about you? Did you get radiation poisoning that has hurt your vision?" She was lying on the couch opposite of Peter. Peter saw her just fine.

"Sorry. I'm just a little startled from the call."

Piper sat up and swung her feet off the couch. "What happened? What's wrong?"

"The Israelis tracked those men down. The ones you thought were family."

Piper leaned forward. "And were they?"

"The Israelis don't know. But they found where

they were staying, and you weren't the only one on their hit list. They were going after an older couple, too."

"They were?" Piper asked.

Peter nodded. "And the older couple is your parents. Piper, the Israelis discovered who you are."

It turned out that Piper's parents lived in a small ranch house in San Francisco. They had been there all the time. It was hard to imagine that she had searched the world for her identity, and it could have been discovered with a short walk.

"Are you ready?" Peter asked Piper. He had parked their car in front of her parents' small house.

"I don't know."

She hadn't talked to her parents yet. She had cowardly asked Peter to call them when they were on their way back to San Francisco. He told Piper's mother on the phone that Piper was fine and that she wanted to see her. Her mother wept with relief, and they set a time to visit the next day.

Peter had decided not to tell Piper's parents about her abduction and her amnesia because he felt that it would be too much of a shock on the phone. He didn't get any more information from them about Piper's past because, again, he thought it would be better to have that conversation in person.

Adesh promised to do a deep background search on Piper's parents just as soon as he prepared for his date with Lola. In the meantime, Piper and Peter would visit her parents.

But they had been sitting in the car in front of Piper's parents' house for the past fifteen minutes, and Piper couldn't bring herself to leave the car.

"Everything I want to know is in that little house," Piper said, pointing at the house. "But now I'm not sure if I want to know what I want to know. You know?"

"Yes, I know."

"I'm scared."

"You defused an atomic bomb with only seconds to spare, but you're afraid of meeting your parents. That sounds about right. My mother once made me pee my pants."

Piper rolled her eyes. "That's a lie."

"A lie to help you, like when I lie about not being able to get my zipper undone so I can get you to cop a feel."

"Believe it or not, I figured out that you were lying about that a long time ago," Piper said. "Okay. I think I'm ready."

Peter opened his door and sprinted around the car and opened Piper's door for her. "Come on, my love. Let's see who you really are."

She leaned in close and buried her head in his muscular chest. "I don't want whatever I'm about to learn to change anything between us."

"Me either."

"I love this, you and me. What if I find out that I'm married? What if I have four kids?"

"With your body? I don't think you've had four kids. As for the husband, I know how to kill him in twenty-eight ways without getting caught, so I'm not totally worried."

"Maybe we should turn around and go home," she whispered.

"No. My Piper doesn't run away from danger. She runs straight into it, face first. Come on. Get your face into that house and meet your folks."

Piper held Peter's hand, glad for his support. They went up the walkway, and Peter rang the doorbell. Piper's mother answered almost immediately.

With just one look, it was obvious that the woman opening the door was Piper's mother. She was a couple of inches shorter, but she had the same aquiline nose and long red hair as Piper. When her mother saw her, she sniffed twice and threw her arms around Piper, giving her a big hug.

The hug made Piper uncomfortable. She half-expected that her memory would flood back when she saw her parents, but it hadn't. She didn't recognize her mother, and she didn't feel inclined to hug her back.

"Let her in, Martha, before you suffocate the poor girl," a man said behind Piper's mother.

He had to be Piper's father. He was tall, and his hair was as red as hers and her mother's. Piper's mother moved aside, and Piper walked into the house.

Her father's eyes filled with tears, and he enveloped Piper in his strong arms. "There's my girl. We nearly died with worry. Where have you been, my sweet girl?"

He looked more familiar to her, but she was still uncomfortable with his hug. Peter put his hand out to shake their hands. "I'm Peter, Piper's friend," he said.

He was smart to describe himself only as her friend. If Piper had been married, he wouldn't want to tell them that he was her boyfriend. They were invited to sit at the kitchen table, and Piper's mother began to boil water at the stove for tea.

"Where have you been? We've been worried sick," her mother said.

"It's sort of a long story," Piper said and looked at Peter for support. He smiled at her and took her hand under the table. "I kind of lost my memory."

"What do you mean?" her father asked.

"She has amnesia," Peter said. "She suffered a trauma that left her without her memory."

Piper's parents exchanged a pointed look. Piper's mother furrowed her eyebrows. "Amnesia?" she asked Piper. "No memory at all?"

"She's lying," Piper's father said.

"She's not lying," Peter said.

"I'm not lying," Piper said. "Why would I lie about something like that? I don't remember who I am. My past is a black hole."

"She's not lying. I can tell that she's telling the truth," Piper's mother said and laughed.

"This is good," her father said. "This way we know she didn't talk."

Piper was confused. The conversation wasn't going the way she had thought it would. "What's going on? Talk about what?"

"Talk or no talk, we can't let them leave," her mother said.

Piper's father, pulled out a long wire from his pocket and pulled it tight in front of himself. He stepped toward her with a menacing expression on his face.

"What the hell?" Peter said.

Piper's mother turned around in the kitchen,

revealing a butcher knife in her hand. "Don't worry. This won't take long," she said.

"Man, you've got some major family issues, Piper," Peter said.

That was an understatement. "Maybe I was a rotten teenager. Maybe I snuck out on Saturday nights," she said.

Piper's father lunged for her with the wire, but Peter intercepted him, punching him in the face. Piper's father went down, but he wasn't down for long. He launched himself at Piper again. Piper ran out of the kitchen, and Peter kicked Piper's father in the back. He screamed in pain.

"Get out of the house!" Peter yelled at Piper.

She moved toward the front door, but her mother was on her heels with the butcher knife. Peter punched her, and she swung her arm, slicing Peter's hand.

"Wow, they really don't like you!" Peter yelled.

He began to do his James Bond maneuvers against them. They weren't a match for him, and when he had them beat, they ran out the back door. A moment later, Piper heard a car screech away.

Peter and Piper sat on the couch and tried to figure out what had just happened.

"I must have been a horrible teenager. Maybe I dealt drugs. Maybe I stabbed my mother, and she wanted to get back at me," Piper said.

"Maybe you poisoned your father's beer. Maybe you kidnapped children and forced them to do your homework." Peter shrugged. "It's anyone's guess."

Piper looked around at the house for the first time. "There are no photos here. Have you noticed that?" she asked Peter.

"Something's fishy in Denmark, that's for sure."

After they searched every drawer and cupboard, they sat back at the kitchen table. "They didn't come back," Piper noted.

"After trying to kill their daughter, you mean? No, I guess they decided to give you a little space."

Piper took a deep breath and replayed everything that had happened in her mind. "What're we thinking? They're not my parents, right?"

Peter nodded. "Even if they're the worst parents in the world, they're not your parents. Nobody lives in this house."

"You can tell because there's no photos?"

"No, I can tell because there's no pots and pans. I can tell because there are shirts and pants in the closet but no underwear in the drawers. I can tell because the house is tidy, but there's a thick layer of dust on everything, as if no one has been here for a very long time. This house is a front. A cover. Those two people are professional killers, and definitely not your parents."

Piper felt a wave of disappointment and relief at the same time. "How do you know for sure? How do you know that they're not my parents? Maybe my parents are professionals. Maybe my parents are homicidal maniacs."

Peter kissed her. "Impossible. Nobody who knows you could ever wish you harm. No matter how screwed up your real parents might be, there's no way that they wouldn't love you."

"Am I ever going to find them? Will I ever know who I am?"

"No," Peter said and then laughed. "Just kidding. Of course, you will. First, I'm going to call in some forensics pals to completely go over this place. That should get us somewhere."

Piper wasn't so sure. A lot of people wanted her dead, and they had resources. They would know how to cover their tracks, too.

Piper moved to get up, and her hand slipped between the couch cushions. She felt something there, and she pulled it out.

"What is it?" Peter asked.

"Matchbox. And look at this." She showed it to him. It was written in Cyrillic, and she translated it for Peter. "*Raven's Nest*. It's a restaurant in Moscow." A memory flashed through her mind.

A restaurant. A man without a face.

That was all she could remember. It was only a brief moment in time, but she held onto it.

"I've been there," she told Peter. "I've been to this restaurant."

"You found a clue and got some of your memory back. That's almost worth getting almost-killed, again."

Peter's hand dripped blood on the carpet, and Piper dug some Kleenex out of her purse and handed it to him.

"You need stitches," she told him. "And a tetanus shot."

"May I have ice cream after?"

"Sure. And I'll help you open your zipper if it gets caught."

EPILOGUE

"I'm scared. What if they don't like me?" Piper asked Peter in the car.

"Impossible. They're going to love you. Not as much as I love you, but pretty close."

"I don't have a good history with parents."

"Only fake parents. My parents are going to smother you with love. My mom's going to see you and picture her future grandkids." They had driven down to San Diego so that Peter could introduce Piper to his parents. He had never been as excited as he was about showing off the woman he loved.

"But what if I disappoint them? What if they think that I'm not good enough for their son?"

"Well, then my mother will stab you with a

butcher knife, and my father will strangle you with a wire. Come on, my mother's watching us through the front window." His mother waved wildly at them and he could see her hopping up and down on her heels. She was very excited about the visit. After all, it was the first time that Peter had ever brought home a woman for them to meet.

"Don't leave me alone in the house. Not for a moment," Piper pleaded with him.

"Deal," Peter said.

They got out of the car. Peter's mother opened the house's front door and squealed with glee. "There's my boy!" she called. "And is that gorgeous girl your sweetheart?"

"She is! Isn't she wonderful? Am I your favorite son now?" Peter called.

"I don't know because Spencer visits more often," she said. "But if you promise to visit more, maybe I'll move you up on the roster."

When they got to the front door, she turned to Piper and gave her a big hug. Piper hugged her back and smiled wide. "I made my world-famous Tater Tot casserole. You're going think you died and went to heaven."

"Really?" Peter asked, excited. "Tater Tot casserole is my favorite."

"And chocolate worms for dessert," his mother

announced.

Peter hopped up and down on his heels. "That means I'm your favorite! I knew it. Spencer can suck it!"

The visit went without a hitch. Piper warmed to Peter's parents immediately, and his parents loved Piper as much as he knew they would. Lunch was delicious, and Piper ate two helpings of the Tater Tot casserole. Meeting his parents made their relationship even more real for him. She was now part of his family, and he wanted to make it official.

Peter palmed the ring box in his pocket. He had picked out the ring the week before they had returned home from Berlin. He had been too nervous to propose, but after seeing how comfortable she was with his parents, he couldn't contain himself any longer. Piper deserved a romantic, elaborate proposal, but he felt the need to ask her now.

"Where's the bathroom?" Piper asked his father, and he showed her to the guest bathroom down the hall.

Peter gave her a couple of minutes and then walked down the hallway, too. "I'm so glad you're here with me," he said through the closed door. "You know how much I love you, and there's something I want to ask you. I'm worried about your answer, but I have to ask you. The thing is that I want to spend the rest of my life with you, and I hope that you'll consider…well, this is stupid to do this through a door. Piper? Are you okay? Mom's Tater Tot casserole has a way of clogging up the pipes. Are you having trouble? My dad's got prune juice in the fridge. Do you want me to get you some?" There was silence. She didn't respond.

"Piper? Piper?" Peter called.

Nothing.

"You're not being attacked again, are you? You don't have a lot of luck with bathrooms," he said and opened the door.

The bathroom was empty. A breeze blew in through an open window. Piper's purse was on the bathroom counter, but there was no sign of her.

Piper had vanished.

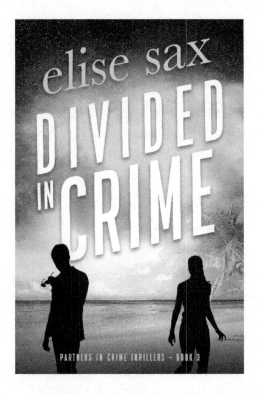

Make sure to sign up for the <u>newsletter</u> to find out about new releases. The next book in the Partner in Crime Thrillers series is: *Divided in Crime*.

ABOUT THE AUTHOR

Elise Sax writes hilarious happy endings. She worked as a journalist, mostly in Paris, France for many years but always wanted to write fiction. Finally, she decided to go for her dream and write a novel. She was thrilled when *An Affair to Dismember*, the first in the *Matchmaker Mysteries* series, was sold at auction.

Elise is an overwhelmed single mother of two boys in Southern California. She's an avid traveler, a swing dancer, an occasional piano player, and an online shopping junkie.

Friend her on Facebook: facebook.com/ei.sax.9
Send her an email: elisesax@gmail.com
You can also visit her website: elisesax.com
And sign up for her newsletter to know about new releases and sales: elisesax.com/mailing-list.php

Printed in Great Britain
by Amazon

44777532R00126